SEX-Esteem

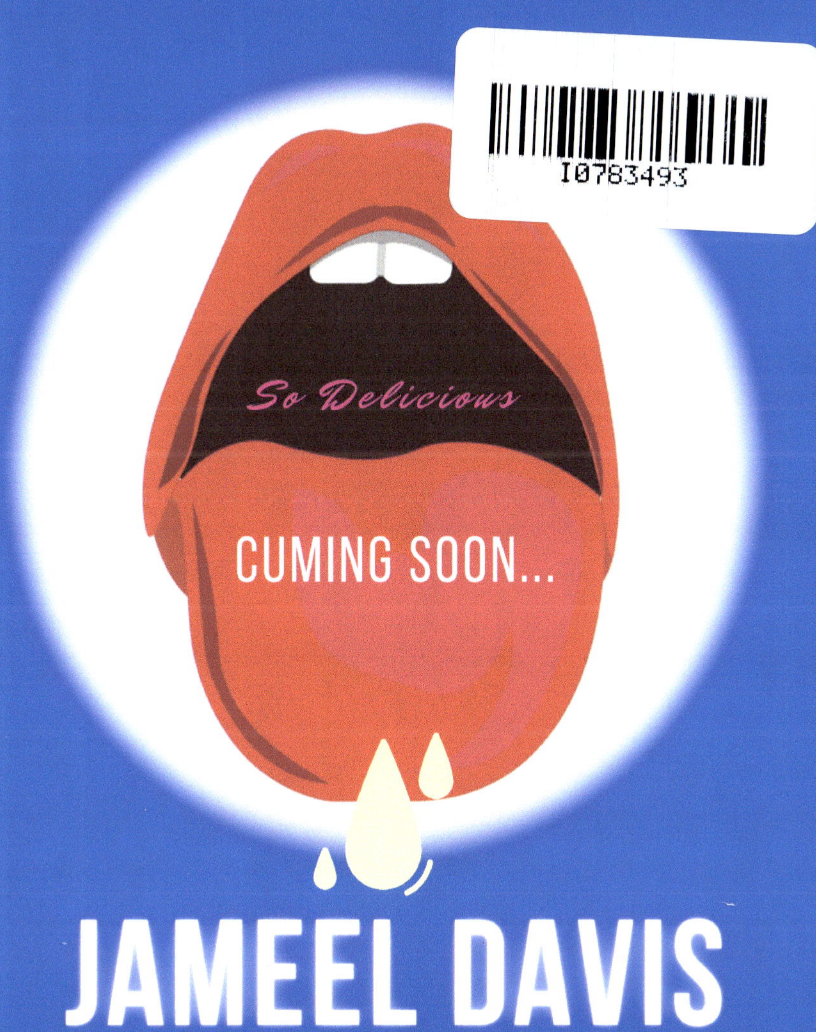

JAMEEL DAVIS

Sex-Esteem

ONE FISH, TWO FISH
PINK FISH, BLUE FISH

KNICK KNACK
KITTY CAT

FEED HER CAT MY BONE

FEBRUARY 14, TWO THOUSAND TWENTY-THREE

YEP! JUST IN TIME.

HER VAGINA IS SMELLIN' FINE.

PRACTICE SAFE SEX

BY PROTECTING YOURSELF AGAINST UNPLANNED PREGNANCY AND SEXUALLY TRANSMITTED INFECTIONS LIKE, CHLAMYDIA, GONORRHEA, SYPHILIS, MYCOPLASMA GENITALIUM, HIV OR HEPATITIS B.

Condoms offer the best available protection against STIs and unplanned pregnancy by acting as a physical barrier to prevent the exchange of semen, vaginal fluids or blood between partners. Like other barrier methods, they are not 100 percent effective in preventing STIs). But they do offer the best protection when used correctly.

When Should I Use a Condom?

- It is really important that you use a condom if you have penis-in-vagina, anal, and oral sex. That way you decrease the chances of contracting sexually transmitted infections and unplanned pregnancy. Ladies, you should use condoms on vibrators and other penetrative sex toys as well.

- Always use a new, lubricated condom every time you have sex. Check the use-by date and open the packet, being careful not to tear the condom with fingernails, jewelry or teeth.

● Condom Effectiveness

- To be effective, condoms must be used from the start of sex to the very end as STIs can be transmitted via pre-ejaculate.

- If stored improperly and water-based lubricant isn't used, the condom may break. It's imperative that you do not use a condom that has been prolonged to heat, that is past its use date, and that has oil-based lubricant applied to it. Condoms are designed for single use only, so please do not attempt to re-apply one that you have already used.

● When Should I Use a Dental Dam?

A dental dam, which is a sheet of latex worn over the female genitals, should be used during oral sex.

● When Should I Use a Diaphragm?

A cap worn high in the vagina to cover the cervix is called a diaphram and it should be worn during penis-in-vagina sex. The diaphragm provides some protection against pregnancy and low protection against STIs.

ADDITIONAL TIPS FOR SAFER SEX

- Take note that alcohol and drugs may affect your ability to make good decisions. So take proper precautions and protect yourself from having sex that you might regret or were pressured into because you were not thinking properly.

- Use other contraception in addition to a condom to avoid unplanned pregnancy.

Jameel Davis

- Be prepared for safe sex – it doesn't have to be a passion-killer. Carry condoms in your wallet or purse and keep them handy at home, so that you don't have to interrupt having sex to look for one.

- If you find condoms reduce the pleasure that you or your partner experience, drop a bit of water-based lubricant in the tip of the condom for extra feeling and sensitivity.
- Learn how to use condoms. They may take a little getting used to, but it's better than catching an STI.
- Involve condoms in foreplay.
- If you feel too embarrassed to buy condoms in a pharmacy or supermarket, buy them from vending machines in some public toilets, from mail-order sites or grab a handful from a community health centre or sexual health centre.
- Hormonal contraceptives, such as the oral contraceptive pill, only provide protection against unplanned pregnancy. They provide no protection against STIs.

- Prioritize your sexual health – it is important.
- Don't think you can tell if someone has an STI just by looking at them. Most STIs don't have any obvious signs.
- Educate yourself about STIs. Anyone who has sex is at risk.
- Be mature about STIs and reassure yourself and your partner that an STI is not a moral judgment of character, but an infection like any other. Having an STI does not mean that you are 'dirty' or 'cheap'.
- Have STI tests if you are in a relationship and you want to have sex without a condom. Both partners should be tested. Think of STI testing as a sign of respect for each other.

Jameel Davis

SPONSORED By
bcondoms

THE FIRST BLACK-OWNED, VEGAN FRIENDLY, ODORLESS & TRIPLE TESTED CONDOM COMPANY OUT OF ATLANTA, GA.

This is a work of fiction. Although its form is that of an autobiography, it is not one. Many stories reflect the author's present recollections of intimate experiences over time which makes it an Erotica memoir as well. The fictional dramatization of the stories enclosed are based on real events as well as the author's pure imagination. For dramatic and narrative purposes, this book contains fictionalized scenes, composite and representative characters and dialogue, and time compression. Names, characteristics, settings and events have been rearranged and changed to suit the convenience of the book and to respect individuals privacy. Certain views and opinions expressed in this book are those of the characters only and do not necessarily reflect or represent the views and opinions held by individuals on which those characters are based. Any resemblance to persons living or dead is coincidental.

Printed in the United States of America

Cover Designer: Jameel Davis

Editor: Stacey M. Robinson, KYA Publishing
Illustrations: Michael Yeboah (Wofa Smallville), Ashley Mae Pancho
Page Designer: Sana Liaqat

Publisher: ElevatedWaves Publishing Corp.
(Garfield Heights, OH)

ISBN-13 (Paperback): 979-8-9867114-0-9
ISBN-13 (Paperback): 979-8-9867114-2-3
ISBN-13 (eBook): 979-8-9867114-1-6

Library of Congress Control Number: 2022943892

First Edition

Davis' books may be purchased in bulk for promotional, educational, or business use. Please contact your local bookseller or ElevatedWaves Publishing at ElevatedWavesPublishing@gmail.com

For more information regarding publicly for author interviews,
email Jameel Davis at jdavi122@kent.edu

WE ARE NO LONGER DEPRIVING OURSELVES FOR WHAT IT IS WE WANT, NEED & DESIRE WHEN IT COMES TO SEX.

#SHEETSCRIPPINGGOOD

Sex-Esteem is a mouthwatering treat for Black women across the world. I have dedicated this book to them—featuring only them inside, without using obscene and abusive language—instead language used to paint the beautiful women they are in a creative, tasteful, and fun erotic fashion. Black women will enjoy this Erotica Memoir and collection of Erotica stories written specially for their sexual satisfaction.

11

YOU CAN'T BE GROWN AND SCARED TO EXPRESS YOURSELF — SEXUALLY!

That's What Your Body is
Made For - Ecstasy

Jameel Davis

GROWN FOLKS DON'T SNEAK AROUND TO DO ADULT THINGS, THAT'S WHAT TEENS DO. YOU'RE GROWN, AREN'T YOU?

So then show me...

13

Jameel Davis

Table of
CONTENTS

03 GAG & GO

04 TWO CAN PLAY THAT GAME — 132

05 LICK IT UP DADDY — 162

ACKNOWLEDGEMENTS — 208

*INDICATES MY FAVORITE ENTRIES

PREFACE

FUCK A PREFACE

SOMETIMES YOU JUST HAVE TO JUMP RIGHT ON-IN-IT TONGUE FIRST,

especially when it's already Wet-and-Ready For you

BUT, I AM GOING TO GIVE YOU ONE ANYWAY...

19

Jameel Davis

Hello and welcome to
SEX-ESTEEM

I have finally decided to give you all what you were anticipating when you first heard of In Between These Sheets and Completely Naked. I appreciate your patience because many of you were very pleased with the plethora of knowledge and wisdom I secreted on those sheets. This time around, I am not playing on words to mind-fuck you with my titles. I am giving you exactly what you are anticipating; creative, hot, sexy, tasteful, intensifying, entertaining, and unfiltered sexual content, with a hint of motivation.

Whether you have purchased this book on your own, borrowed it, or received it as a gift from a friend, colleague, or loved one, I would like to thank you for trusting me with your investment of time, money, patience, and intimate energy.

Before we begin, I must first inform you that I am no Zane or any of the other known erotic novelists. Nor is it my aim to become an erotic novelist. I am simply just testing the waters in a fun and intimate way with the aim to please those who yearn for orgasmic pleasures. I have my own way with words and experiences, which you will soon discover here in Sex-Esteem.

Although many of the sheets herein will create sexual arousal, being the man I am, I cannot proceed without first touching on the importance of sex in the Black community and why healthy and satisfying heterosexual sex is important for the advancement of the Black culture.

Healthy, safe, wild, crazy, passionate, adventurous, and nasty sex with a profound Black woman is beautiful;

it tastes beautiful, feels beautiful, looks beautiful, sounds beautiful, and even smells beautiful. I wouldn't have it any other way.

It's human nature for man and woman to express themselves sexually with one another, but there are many adults (especially those who make up the Black professional and religious communites) who are ashamed to openly talk about good ole, healthy, nasty, and beautiful sex...some of which they sneak to watch, read, listen to, and perform when no one is watching. For me, it's no big secret of mine; I love to bring extreme sexual satisfaction to my Black woman in various ways and places, and to express it as loudly as we possibly can, both orally and literary. Whichever critic on the outside becomes a witness to the erotica scenes I paint and engage in, can just keep on watching, reading, and talking their talk because to me, sex with a beautiful, educated, feminine, and strong Black woman is necessary, healthy, magical, and electrifying.

BLACK SATISFYING HETEROSEXUAL SEX SHOULD BE HIGHLIGHTED WITHOUT SHAME AND REGARD WITHIN THE BLACK COMMUNITY, BECAUSE IT IS A VERY SATISFYING WORK OF ART — TWO OF THE WORLD'S GREATEST HUE-MAN BEINGS DEMONSTRATING HOW THEIR BLACK ANCESTORS CREATED THE HUMAN RACE WITH JOY AND PLEASURE, AND HOW IT IS HUMAN NATURE FOR MAN AND WOMAN TO PROCREATE, AND/OR ENJOY ONE ANOTHER IN SUCH A MANNER.

Images and literature of dominant Black men and women, loving on one another in an intimate way needs to be shown, because right now all we are observing are images of us tearing each other apart: on television, inside of our households, and in our communities.

Many Black professionals in the Black and religious communities are quick to show, teach, and promote everything except enjoyable sex: financial literacy, real estate, life skills, sports, music, gardening, fashion, hair, cosmetics, violence, and so forth. It's like they are afraid that it will ruin their reputation, causing them to lose in life or something.

Knowing that enjoyable heterosexual Black sex is hidden from the public eye in our communities, many Black adults (especially women) have never experienced it, and have no clue as to where to begin to receive it.

Jameel Davis

Many are trapped in unsatisfying sexual relationships and marriages, with no willpower and courage to escape:

> *"Her partner lays on top of her and finishes his business proudly, leaving her with no excitement on her end. She believes sex is only for the pleasure of man, because he has never brought her to ecstasy— and most likely he hasn't, because he has never been taught how."*
>
> *"She begins to enjoy his thrusting penetration, he stops, forces her to turn around and finishes in her mouth or on her face, never returning the favor — and/or he finishes way too soon, with no ammunition or desire to bring her to climax."*
>
> *"She's not aroused, she doesn't want it; yet he forces himself inside of her anyway."*

That is a selfish, yet a horrible way to live! Sex is for the pleasure of both man and woman; his aim should be to please her and her aim should be to please him until satisfaction has been reached.
Sex without consent is RAPE.

"She desperately wants to have sex and reach the big "O" her girlfriends are always celebrating about. She's alone and not brave enough to approach the man she desires, so she searches her high school classroom in exchange for passing grades."

Jameel Davis

Many Black people are angry today, because they aren't — and don't know how to—have satisfying sex. This is why images and literature promoting fun and healthy Black sex needs to be shown in our communites by the way of Black men and women loving on one another in an intimate way. Satisfying sex helps keep your immune system humming, boosts self-esteem, lowers your blood pressure, eases stress, lessens pain, improves sleep, and decreases depression and anxiety, all which are major health problems that are troubling the Black community.

Although I'm unable to show you live images of my sexual activity here due to respect, public policy, privacy acts, and laws surrounding publishing such content, I have painted scenes herein through my creative imagination and descriptive writing for your reference and leisure.

Outside of kicking inspiration and motivation to people from various backgrounds, traveling, signing books, managing my career, educating myself, planning ahead, goofing around, and spending time with those who matter most, I'm coloring outside of the lines — creating magical sexual moments with my Black woman wherever the excitement takes me...whether it be on the High Roller, the back of a jet ski, in the dark woods behind the cabin, in a paddle boat on the lake, the back of a golf cart at the sixth and ninth hole, on the left wing of a jet aircraft, *or In Between These Sheets.*

Jameel Davis

You should be marking off your sexual fantasy bucket list as well, without shame and regard.

*"If she wants to feel your tongue twirling in circles on her clitoris, outside in the middle of the day, place her on the hood of your car and BURY YOUR MOUTH DEEP INSIDE OF HER WITHOUT QUESTION. Forget what your boys think, or what the pastor may think. **CLEAN YOUR PLATE & CLEAN IT GOOD UNTIL SHE BEGS YOU TO STOP.** And even then, don't stop until your stomach is full."*

"The back of your throat has an itch that needs to be relieved by the head of his swollen dick, put your tonsils to the side and get to work on the balcony of your Las Vegas suite. Forget what your jealous aunty and girlfriends have to say. Suck it crazy, gag on it until you can't breathe — cry tears of joy, then slide it back and forth against your throbbing clit, then into the mouth of your hungry puma."

"It's sundress season and you are out walking in the park with bae. Mommy breeze does you a favor and gives him a peek of your bare, golden-brown bottom. You left your lace panties in your top drawer just for him, and the swings are free; why not race to the stars together?

Sit him on the swing, take a seat and fly high together."

HERE IS SEX-ESTEEM, WRITTEN FOR YOU. I HOPE YOU ENJOY YOUR "WET READ" AND I CAN'T WAIT TO MEET YOU DRY ON THE OTHER SIDE.

P.S. - PLEASE DO NOT HIDE THIS BOOK IN FRONT OF A MAGAZINE, NEWSPAPER, OR ANOTHER BOOK. JUST BE YOURSELF.

#CULTIVATINGMINDS — BE WHO YOU ARE WHEN THE CAMERA IS ROLLING AS YOU ARE WHEN IT'S OFF. EVEN IF IT MEANS GETTING A LITTLE NASTY OUTSIDE OF THESE SHEETS.

I WOULDN'T BE ME IF I WASN'T NASTY...

LET THE FUN BEGIN

Jameel Davis

A-FUN-FACT

WHEN I WAS JUST A TEENAGE BOY IN HIGH SCHOOL, I THOUGHT GOING DOWN ON A FEMALE WAS THE MOST DISGUSTING THING EVER.

TURNS OUT, I WASN'T DOING IT RIGHT.

NOW,
I CAN'T KEEP MY MOUTH
OFF OF HER EXTRA SET OF LIPS,
AND THEY CAN'T STOP KISSING ME.

28

Jameel Davis

Creed Aventus Cologne

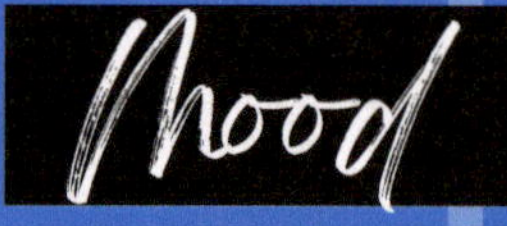

Palms Place Las Vegas

Red Smoke Jacket, Black Slacks, Slippers

Champagne, Cigar, Chocolates

Sex Room by Ludacris

Scan & Listen

WELCOME TO MY SEX ROOM

WHERE EACH PAGE IS SHEETS-GRIPPING-GOOD!

Jameel Davis

GILDAN
GILDAN

Welcome To My Sex Room

Jameel Davis

Welcome To My Sex Room

Jameel Davis

Scan & Listen

SIP & PAINT

I'm in no race or competition to prove who can serve you better. I'm just here to let you know my touch is strictly reserved for me.

See, sex is a form of art and I am a gestural abstraction and graffiti artist. I am the brush to your canvas and the spray paint to your river mural. Once I insert my brush into your palette of paint, my only desire is to complete your portrait — spontaneously dribbling, splashing, and smearing your paint, while gliding my body onto your canvas until satisfaction has been reached.

I am not here to just wet my brush.

This spray can of mine will turn your walls into breathtaking waterfalls that you and I would often want to visit, like Niagara.

See, not only is the touch of my brush magical, so is my timing and affection. As you enjoy the thrill of me being with and inside you, I will be checking your vitals to breathe at the same rate as you, to gasp and moan with you.

DURING OUR BREATHING INTERVALS, I WILL BE PASSIONATELY LICKING, SUCKING, AND KISSING ALL ON YOUR STERNOCLEIDOMASTOID, BREASTS, AND LIPS, ALONG WITH EACH STROKE OF MY BRUSH UNTIL YOU BEGIN TO LOSE CONTROL AND ERUPT

Jameel Davis

As you are covering me with your
April showers, I will be looking at
you with excitement, deeply into
your eyes, smiling at your
expressions of satisfaction.

Wow! Look at my work.

You will be my canvas, and at this point you will be
secured on my easel: no getting free. The strokes of my
brush will begin to flow rapidly, increasing the rate of
our simultaneously beating hearts.

Our synch gasps and moans will become more and
more intense, as I time your next eruption to erupt with
you, creating a very valuable work of art.

A famous portrait will be made.

I want to create another one right after.

Only this time, you be the painter.

Dip my brush into your cup of water, then into your palette
of paint, and begin softly stroking the bristles onto your
blank canvas.

Turn your dry canvas into a magical waterfall when you
submerge my brush deeper into your sparkling blue.

PAINT A PICTURE OF A RIVER FLOWING BEAUTIFULLY IN THE HORIZON.

Jameel Davis

Before I had you secured on my easel...now secure my easel in you, and keep me near you until your portrait is complete. When you release your grip, I will know that magic and fireworks have been made again, in my Magic Kingdom.

So yes, It Is Worth It, You Can Work It. Put Your Thing Down, Flip It and Reverse It.

NOW LETS BOOST YOUR SEX-ESTEEM!

GIVE IT A TRY

Fellas, stop in mid-missionary-stroke and race your head down between her thighs in the middle of her gasp or moan — press and twirl your tongue up against her swollen clitoris, and suck on it (slowly with passion) for about 30 seconds.

 Then, stop to slide the head of your erect dick back inside of her creamy pussy — serving her slow, deep, smooth, and rapid strokes.

 Then, stop in mid-stroke again, holding her legs wide open, slurping on her swollen clitoris fast, slowly and soft until she reaches the urge to climax.

 Then, race to insert your dick back inside for her to cum all over it.

Her Body's Response to this Ecstasy should be Electrifying.

*I don't always make it back inside on time. Sometimes she just finishes on my tongue and I re-enter afterwards. But, the challenge of timing her orgasm while I'm down below and trying to race the head of my dick back inside, pressing it against her throbbing clit as she is cuming is always a thrill.

Jameel Davis

RAIN-DOWN-ON-ME

Over the last month and a half, I've nearly awakened in the morning, afternoon, and in the night with the most intense erections ever— with the head of my dick making a tent in my boxers. Trying to escape into the warm, wet, and slimy regions of her. I mean I've been so hard, so aroused, that if she locked eyes with the head of my swollen dick, this volcano of mine would have exploded everywhere. All over myself.

"Who said shower chairs are only for the elderly and the disabled?" I thought to myself.

"Rain-Down-On-Me is what I had envisioned from her water spout over the last month and a half; but she was nowhere near; she was a fantasy in my mind."

So I prepped the shower for an intense virtual water show performance.

Pulling back the shower curtain, I picked up the gray shower bench and placed it in the center of the shower, directly beneath the shower head. I then set the water temperature to hot and stepped out of my tent shaped boxers, kicking them off to the side. Before stepping into the hot and steamy shower, I looked down and admired my beautiful brown headliner and watched as he prepared himself for ecstasy — extending and thickening himself with the thought of our virtual shower chair performance.

40

Jameel Davis

and I followed in right after. Before taking a seat on the gray shower bench, I rinsed the morning off of me and cleansed my body right after.

 I took my seat and allowed the hot water to Rain-Down-On-Me and my semi-fully-erect dick.

Jameel Davis

I took my dick into my right hand and stroked it several times underneath the hot water. My upper body was in the way of the water falling directly onto my dick, so I leaned back on the bench to give my dick the star attention he needed while still holding him firmly in my hand. I pulled my dick up toward my stomach and slowly...

"...stroked
and I watched her stroke,
and I stroked,
and I watched her stroke,
and I stroked

and I watched her stroke me inside of her slimy, wet, and warm body, until he fully extended and widened himself, and his head swelled like a mushroom cap, ejaculating his creamy love all down the sides of himself.

Love washed off of me and down the drain like the visual I had of her straddling me on the shower stool like she had done several times before.

"Only this time it was just me."

Chapter 1

"Tales from the Clit"

"TALES FROM THE CLIT"

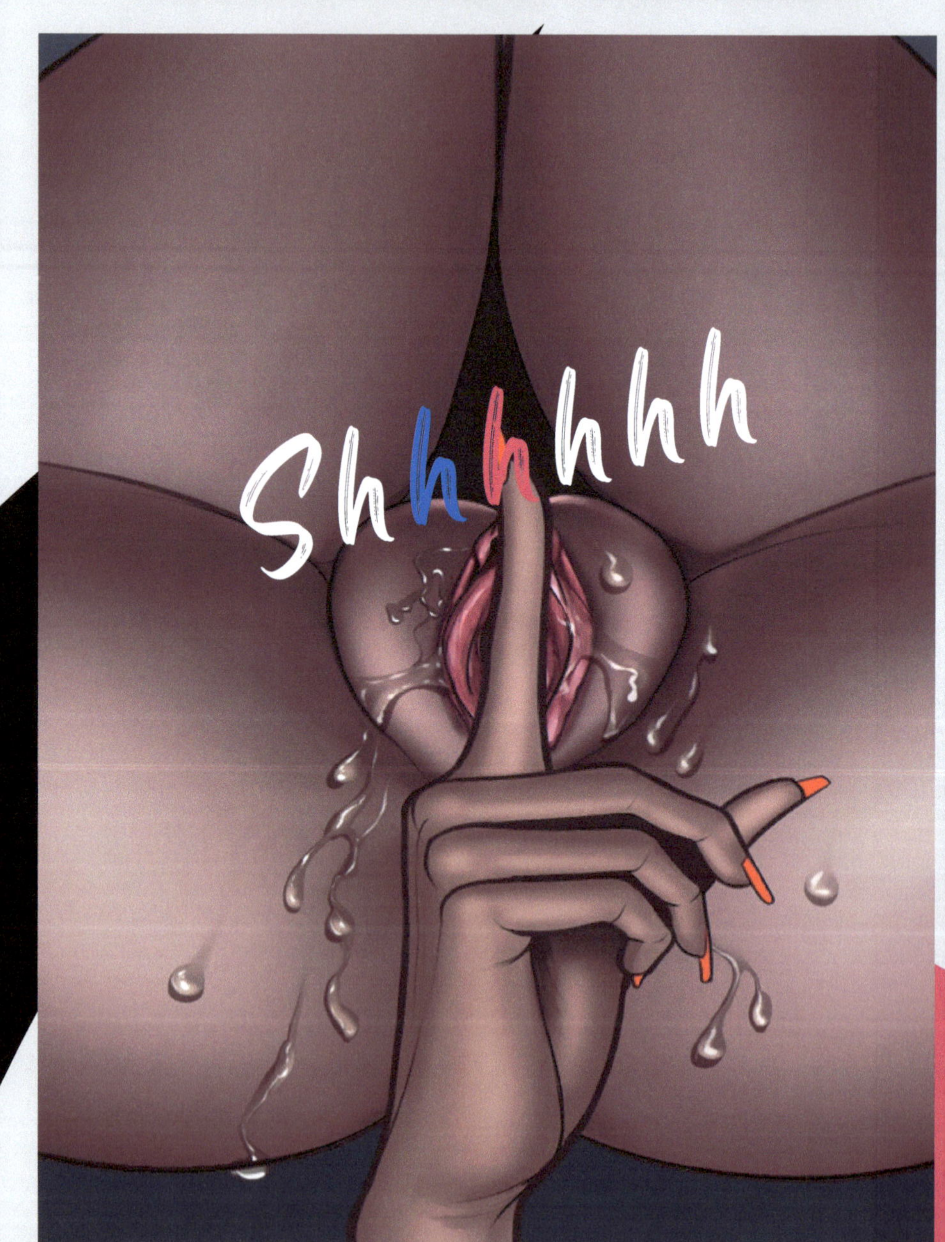

THE QUICKER-PICKER-UPPER

She studied me as I sat comfortably on a black spandex banquet chair right in front of her, sporting my black velvet blazer, slowly sucking scampi off of wooden skewers.

She watched as I licked and sucked the alfredo sauce that fell from each scampi onto my lips, right off of my lips.

I was always told that I have nice lips, so I make sure I keep them smooth and moist — for special kisses.

I never knew she was watching me. I was really hungry.

"Mmm you did that good," she acknowledged with a flirtatious smile after lightly tapping me on my right shoulder.

Remembering to not talk with my mouth full, I surveyed her body language as she locked eyes with me, held her smile, and waited for me to clear my mouth.

While chewing up the last bits of the scampi so I could swallow and respond, I watched as she crossed her legs and squeezed her thighs tightly together, trying to hold back the river that was getting ready to form a puddle in her seat.

She indicated to the group earlier, she retired her panties long ago, so I knew the only thing that could catch her falls in the event of a water main break was the black cloth she sat upon.

"Thank you," I said, smiling in return, and licking my lips once more.

"Yeah, I did that and I can do that too," nodding my head in the direction of the river I knew was flowing in between her legs.

I remember, she kept mentioning paper towels with a smirk on her face, crossing and uncrossing her legs throughout the event that evening:

"The Quicker-Picker-Upper - Bounty" we shouted together at one instance.

I didn't know if her river had already started to flow and if she actually needed to wipe her stream of crystal liquids from flowing down her inner thighs and onto her seat at the time.

But now I know all along she wanted me to,"Quickly Pick-Her, Eat Her & Lick-Her Up," like I did the scampi and alfredo sauce.

So I..."

Cactus Blossom by Bath & Body Works

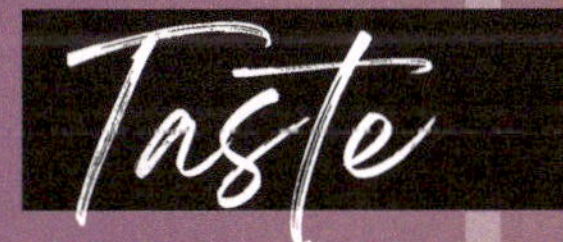

Netflix & Chill

Silk Press, Lip Gloss, Gray T-shirt, No Panties

Ice

Yummy by Justin Bieber

Scan & Listen

ICE CREAM

Imagine getting your hair washed, then BOOM, he starts suckling on and twirling his cool tongue all around your clitoris...

Slowly, close your eyes and open your thighs.

ICE CREAM

  Imagine having nothing on except your towel. You spread your curvy legs and he bends you over, placing your head underneath the warm running water in the sink.

  He slides over to the right, running his fingers through your hair, prepping it for the Olive Oil shampoo he plans to clean each strand of hair with.

  Picture him running his fingers through your hair, getting it all wet, and then _boom, you feel his firm dick through his jeans, pressing up against your soft-round-ass,_ as he reaches to the left and retrieves the shampoo from the countertop.

  Suddenly, you feel his hand gently grab your shoulder and move you back from the water.

  He applies the shampoo to your hair and begins using both of his hands to deeply massage the white-creamy-like liquid in your hair and scalp, hitting those spots better and longer than your favorite hairdresser.

  Imagine after the third wash, while your head is still under the warm water, you feel his wet hands caress your breasts, as he lick and suck on your ear — then kiss and twirl his warm-thick tongue in slow, small circular motions on your neck — sending horny chills throughout your body.

Picture him pausing momentarily to take a drink of ice water, and he place one of the ice cubes in his mouth — kneel down and slide his cold mouth between the back of your thighs— suckling all on your horny clitoris — gliding the ice cube and his tongue across your warm juicy lips — until his ice and your cream melt all over his mouth and face.

Ahhhh! Ice Cream!

P.S. — I am one of the best shampooers in the world!

Book your appointment today!

Beautiful Day by Bath & Body Works

Breakfast in Bed

Fresh out the Shower, Naked Lying On A Towel

Pineapple, Peppermint, Amaretto Sour

Makin' Good Love by Avant

Scan & Listen

SEPARATED

A girl's legs are her best friends and it's time for her best friends to part ways for the arrival of my flipper and submarine — which will soon be submerged deep between them.

Mesmerized by her sexy thighs and soft and lovely lips, I hovered my bare body over Symone's, licked my lips, and gently placed them passionately onto hers. Her body quivered and she squirmed on the flannel sheets, inserting her tongue deep into my mouth.

I tasted the amaretto sour on her tongue from when she sipped on it seconds after tracing her tongue slowly in circular motions down my neck, to my swollen dick and ball-sack. I sucked off the remaining cocktail from her tongue and made love to her juicy bottom lip with my tinder pink lips and talented tongue.

Symone arched her back, gasped and squirmed once more, scooting her delicate cheeks down — opening her legs to feel my horny dick knock at the entrance of her sopping pussy.

I placed my athletic arms around her legs and cuffed her thighs with my palms, pulling her down to the center of the queen size bed, opening them back up.

"I got her friends spread all over the bed
Hands playing with her breasts
Moans loud yeah I know
The only thing on her mind is fucking me."

Resting my hands on Symone's inner thighs, I slowly brought my mouth as close as I could to her leaking lips — blowing them warm kisses. Symone grinded her pelvis in the air reaching for my lips to fasten on her aroused clitoris — her pussy lips blew me a warm kiss back instead.

Replacing my right hand with my tongue on her inner thigh, I slid my hands up to her knees and began alternating her inner thighs with slow kisses and twirling licks.

Working my neck toward her center, I blew circles of cool air onto her clitoris. Symone grinded her pelvis in the air reaching for my lips again. This time, I fastened my lips softly onto her throbbing clit.

Symone inhaled deeply, held her breath, and exhaled slowly — resting her cheeks back onto the sheets.

I opened my mouth and flicked the tip of my tongue full speed up and down Symone's clit and she squirmed out of control. I lifted my head up to see the facial expressions she was making. I smiled in satisfaction.

 Symone caught me looking, grabbed hold of the back of my head with her hand — lifted her pelvic and pressed my mouth firmly back against her sopping lips.

 I licked her lips and clitoris clean. I took her clitoris into my mouth and sucked on it like a peppermint til she screamed in ecstasy — releasing her most intensifying orgasm ever — all in my mouth.

Breakfast was all about her.

I brought her best friends back together until lunch — when I separated them again, submerging my dick deep into her tight, spongy pussy — cumming uncontrollably together.

(Female) Romance by Ralph Lauren, (Male) Jimmy Choo Man by Jimmy Choo

Repent

(Male) Gray Sweats, White T-shirt, (Female) Senegalese Twists/Faux Locs, Pink Lipstick, White Robe

Hershey White Creme, Chocolate Wine

Wild Side by Normani feat. Cardi B

Scan & Listen

BAPTIZE ME

Oh Dear Heavenly Goddess Spirit of Pussy,

 I come before you and deeply ask of you, to forgive me for all of the nasty sins I have committed. I am fully aware of my actions and the damage my flirtatious tongue and talented penis have done to her body — repeated deep, massive, vaginal and clitoris orgasms which removed her happy soul from her body, causing her to become overly obsessive, insecure, and dangerous. It was never supposed to happen that way. I thought we were really bonding and creating magic; she sighed with joy and smiled after each orgasm until her body went limp. She was really a smart and respectful girl until one day she granted me the opportunity to twirl my tongue on her clitoris for breakfast, lunch, and dinner, while serving her long passionate tongue strokes in her southern mouth, until she clenched her legs around my neck, releasing her first ever orgasm all over my face, while choking on my meaty dick. I am deeply sorry for disobeying your 6th and 9th commandments:

6th — "You shalt not use the full potential of your tongue on a virgin clitoris."

9th — "You shalt not snatch the soul from her body with your mouth while her mouth is already full with you."

"Please forgive me oh pussy goddess," I pleaded.

After a moment of self-reflection, I have come to the realization that I should have never disobeyed your commandments, and should have never been worshiping her body before you. I should have been worshiping you and only you.

Oh Heavenly Goddess Spirit of Pussy, I am fully ready to accept you as my Lady and Shepherdess, and as my personal savior, as you have sacrificed your soul and love, time and time again for my sexual pleasures. I recognize and acknowledge you as my true shepherdess and savior, and Oh Heavenly Goddess Spirit of Pussy, I am ready to be baptized in your savoring name and in your milky wet galaxy, and to live righteously inside of you.

"My son, I have heard your prayers which you have released into my atmosphere and I have forgiven you for your sexual sins. For you are my son. Because I am your protector and have protected you with my arousal fluids, and you have accepted me as your lady and personal savior, and have found me to be nourishing and tasteful — I will grant you access into my heaven gates. But, you must first be baptized at Squirt United Missionary. I have arranged your baptism for this Sunday with First-lady Pastor Waters. Please bring something comfortable (like those thin gray sweats I like sitting on you in) that show your nice dick print, and a white t-shirt. Oh, and come showered and alone; this will be a special ceremony for you."

"Thank you, Heavenly Goddess Spirit of Pussy."

"Hello DJ, you look and smell very nice today," Pastor Waters said, as she greeted me at the back door with a tight two-arm hug with no intention of letting me go. Looking over her left shoulder, I could see her pretty round-round that was driving me wild, extending from her backside. That stunning view, plus the Romance aroma by Ralph Lauren (that drifted from her neck into my nostrils) made my dick pulse. I quickly moved my pelvis back and separated myself from her before my dick jerked again. I didn't want her to feel it grow and knock on her stomach.

"I wonder if she felt the first throb before I had the chance to move away?"

I am Pastor Waters, welcome to Squirt United Missionary. I have been expecting you. Pastor Waters wore an ivory silk robe with a short split that stopped three inches above her knees.

She stood about 5'5". She was medium in size with glazed dark chocolate skin, plumped lips colored with plum lipstick, and gloss lip gel. She wore black medium length Senegalese twists that stopped in the middle of her back. She was indeed a Goddess. I could see why she was appointed Head Pastor by the Heavenly Goddess Spirit of Pussy: she was stunning.

"DJ, I have been made aware that you wish to be cleansed of your nasty sins and baptized in my baptistery, so your spirit can go on and live internally through the spirit of the Heavenly Goddess of Pussy," she noted.

"Yes ma'am. That is correct. I have repented and I am ready to be forgiven of my sins. I want to get baptized in her heavenly name."

"That is great. I am happy to know you have found yourself in the spirit of Mother Pussy, and are here to let me baptize you in my baptistery. Please follow me, this way."

Pastor Waters led me down a short narrow hallway. As she walked in front of me like she was walking the runway during New York Fashion Week, her pretty round-round was swaying from side to side, driving me wilder. My dick stretched down my thigh and grew more firm as her robe rose up over each of her chocolate glazed cheeks.

She had nothing beneath it, and she wanted me to know it.

We took a quick left and immediately stepped through an opened door on the right leading into the baptistery.

"Open or closed?" I asked.

"Open, my deaconess will be arriving shortly to assist me."

Pastor Waters stepped into the warm bubbly water with her ivory robe on, and sat her delicate-chocolate-round bottom up on the edge of the cream baptistery facing me, as she would if she was performing a live baptism in front of an audience.

She looked as if she was dipped into Hershey White Creme and I wanted to eat the whole candy bar. I stood before her, awaiting her instructions.

"DJ, did you bring the clothing that was requested of you?" she asked.

"Yes, ma'am; I have them right here in my duffle bag."

"Okay, great. Now, please take off your shoes, your socks, those jeans," she pointed, "that shirt, and your underwear. Then slip into the items you brought with you."

"Right here?" I asked.

"Yes, right here. I won't look," she replied, smiling.

I slowly began removing my articles of clothing in the order she asked me to remove them and sat them on the bench near the door. As I was taking off my gray Hanes boxer-briefs, sliding them off of my right foot, I glanced up to see if she was watching me, and she was. As soon as I caught her eyes studying Mr. Davis Jr., she quickly turned her head away.

I proceeded to unzip my duffle bag that was placed on the floor beside me, and retrieved my thin gray sweats the Heavenly Goddess Spirit of Pussy loved to see me in. I slid them on and threw on my fresh white tee.

"*All done,*" I said with a grin.

"*Now, walk on over and slowly step down into the baptistery. Once you are inside, come on over to where I am sitting.*"

I walked down the four short steps that led me into the water. With each step, the water gradually rose up to my waistband.

"Wait! Back up to the second step," she yelled.

"Why? Did I do something wrong?" I replied.

"No, just stand on the second step for a second. I need to see something."

"Alright."

I walked back onto the second step as the Pastor instructed.

Once I was back on the step, I found her eyes laser-focused on my now see-through gray sweats that fully revealed the print of my resting dick — licking the gel right off her thick juicy lips.

"I know why I was prompted to come alone."

The temperature of the water put my dick in a weakened state as soon as the head of my dick made contact with the water. Had the water been any colder, my dick would have shriveled up.

Loud enough for me to hear her, *"Wet-gray sweats contest and I think we have a winner,"* Paster Waters mumbled.

63

   Pastor Waters flicked her right index finger back and forth, signaling me to come on over to where she was sitting. I treaded the water as I walked on over to where she sat. Inside of the baptistery housed two Jacuzzi seats — for the Pastor and one other person. Pastor Waters slid her bottom off of the edge and scooted down into the seat right beneath where she was sitting. I assumed she wanted me to sit in the seat right beside her, but she didn't ask me to sit. She insisted I keep standing. I then watched her left hand disappear into the water heading south in between her thickset thighs. Her right stiletto fingernail entered the corner of her mouth and rested on a bottom tooth as her eyes quickly undressed me before shutting.

   "Pastor," I yelled, startling her.

   "Yes, DJ," she moaned softly, biting her bottom lip.

   I stood in silence and she slowly opened her eyes. I looked at her and simultaneously tilted my head, opened my palms, and shrugged my shoulders forward, signaling what's next.

   "Oh sorry babe, I had a moment," she cried out. *'We are waiting for my deaconess to come in to assist me with your baptism.'*

"Are you sure you still want to follow through with this?" she asked.

"Yes, I am ready to wash away my sexual sins, cleansing my soul with the spirit of the Heavenly Goddess of Pussy."

Pastor Waters looked up near the entrance and saw a figure standing there smiling. *"Oh hi, Deaconess Brown, come on in and join us. This is DJ, the fine gentleman we have the pleasure of baptizing today."*

Deaconess Brown was short and slim. But she had a nice set of C-cup breasts that sat up nice with curvy hips to match. She was caramel-skinned, with small tinder lips wrapped in pink lipstick. She wore her hair in faux locs that were pinned in a bun on the top of her head.

From where I was standing, the way her matching white robe traced the outline of her body, it looked as if she was bow-legged, with curves that led to something round, soft and plumped on her backside.

There is something about a slim frame that is bow-legged with a nice booty that makes me want to relapse, violating the 6th and 9th commandments. But I snapped out of it and focused back on the real reason for my visit, and that was cleansing my mouth, penis, and

65

spirit of sins I committed against the virgin woman whose life I ruined by bringing her powerful orgasms that trembled her entire body. A feeling she had never experienced and wasn't prepared for.

Deaconess Brown walked over and joined us in the baptistery. She squeezed her D-cup breasts up against my chest as she wrapped her arms around me, snuggling me tight. I damn near nutted on myself. My dick shot up in the quickness, ready to shoot rounds right through my sweats. I glanced down over the back of her right shoulder and there it sat, a golden apple that had unveiled itself when she stretched up to hug me. I pulled back slightly from her, so she wouldn't feel how rock hard my dick had gotten.

"Pleasure to meet you Deaconess Brown, I am happy you are here to assist me with my baptism," I smiled.

"Pleasure to meet you as well DJ. We are going to take good care of you during this ceremony," she grinned, showing her pretty whites that were wired with metal.

"You don't have to worry about a thang, honey."

"I love me a Black woman with a sexy smile and who wears braces," I shouted to myself with excitement.

"DJ, your ceremony shall begin now," moaned Pastor Waters, who was still sitting in her Jacuzzi seat. I looked down into the water where she sat and saw her legs slightly held open, with four of her left handed fingers compressed and rotating in circular motions on her clitoris. My dick instantly swelled more and started throbbing out of control.

Pastor Waters rested her feet up on the seat, widened her legs more, and kept her fingers circling on her clit. She twirled her ass counterclockwise in her seat, gasping quietly.

Pastor Waters spoke softly, *"DJ?"*

"Yes ma'am," I replied.

Deaconess Brown moved closer to the left side of me and supported my lower back with her right hand and slid her left hand beneath the water, gently stroking my dick through my sweats. I was hard as a brick.

My eyes quickly relaxed until Pastor Waters spoke again.

"Do you believe that the Clitoris is the daughter of the Heavenly Goddess of Pussy?" she asked.

"I do."

"Do you believe she has sacrificed her sexual pleasure for your pleasure, and that her happiness is vital in helping you rid your sins and achieving your desires during your time here?"

"Yes Pastor, I strongly believe."

"Do you accept the Heavenly Goddess of Pussy as your Lady and personal savior?"

"Yes Pastor, I do accept the Heavenly Goddess of Pussy as my Lady and personal savior."

Pastor Waters retrieved her left hand from the water and whispered, "Come to me DJ," with her palms out and arms extended, reaching for my hands to lock inside of hers.

I took two steps forward and placed my hands in her small open palms. She widened her thighs and pulled my hands toward her until I was nearly standing in between them. My dick was ready to burst through my sweats and through Deaconess Brown's hand.

He wanted to thrust the inner lining of Pastor Water's and Deaconesses Brown's vagina so badly.

But it wasn't the place for that. He had to get cleansed.

"DJ, the Heavenly Goddess Spirit of Pussy forgives and accepts you. It is time for us to cleanse you entirely in her forgiving waters."

"Place your arms across your chest and kneel down a bit," Pastor Waters begged. I will support your head and Deaconess Brown is going to support the back of your neck and shoulders, as we submerge your body into the water twice.

"Once for the Mother, and once more for the Daughter, and the Holy Goddess Spirit of the Pussy."

Pastor Waters dipped her left hand back into the water and continued massaging her clitoris, moving her body round and round in her seat. Pastor Waters reached up and took hold of the back of my head with her right hand, told me to hold my breath and pulled my head down into the water.

Deaconess Brown took control of my neck and shoulders and they both guided my face between Pastor Waters' thighs, and to her aroused clitoris.

69

My talented tongue rested on her clitoris, as she lifted her ass up from the seat and grinded her clit harder and harder into my tongue. I heard Pastor's loud moan travel swiftly through the water before I was lifted back up for air.

Breathing heavily, she moaned, *"DJ, you have been baptized in the name of the Mother."*

After catching my wind, I was submerged beneath the water once more and I fastened my mouth and tongue back on her smooth clitoris like a button. I started orbiting my flickering tongue around her clit in the same direction they were rotating my head and neck. Pastor Waters rested her left hand on the back of my head along with her right hand. She tugged my head as if she caught a football, and secured my mouth on her thrusting clitoris. Pastor Waters threw her hips round and round, up and down, and back and forth, as I licked the spirit of the Daughter out of her.

She wailed in fulfillment, clenching my head with her thickset thighs, climaxing a slimy crystal gel into the forgiving waters. All of the muscles in her body weakened and my head was set free from her wedge.

Deaconess Brown quickly pulled me from up under the water, wiping away the water from my eyes. When my eyes opened, I caught Pastor Waters sitting on cloud nine.

"*D — J,*" Pastor Waters called out, breathing heavily.

"You have been bap-tized in the name of the Daugh-ter and the Heavenly Goddess...of the Pussy. You have been wiped clean of all your dirty sin.

Pastor Waters slowly rose to her feet and stretched her torso up, wrapping her arms around my neck, embracing me. I wrapped my arms around her waist and placed my hands on the cusp of her plumped-chocolate-round ass that met with the bottom of the robe she wore. I groped her delicate, fluffy cheeks, and lifted them up, pulling her close to me.
I know she felt my fully erect, jerking dick trying to burst through her stomach this time.

"*You have been granted entry into the heaven gates and to the family of the Heavenly Goddess of Pussy. With this baptism, you carry the power of the holy clit and shall be protected in arousal fluid and crystal climax for eternity,*" she exclaimed.

"*Thank you Pastor Waters,*" I said gracefully, with a smile. "*I accept this baptism and will honor and serve the Heavenly Goddess Spirit of Pussy for the rest of my human life.*"

Pastor Waters gradually pulled away from me, guided me to the seat next to hers, and signaled for me to step up and take a seat on the edge of the baptistery. I placed my hands on the edge of the baptistry, stepped my right foot on the seat, pulled myself up on the edge, and sat facing her and Deaconess Brown.

"This day forward, this Jacuzzi seat belongs to you and every Sunday at this hour I want you here," Pastor Waters said in a sexy tone.

Deaconess Brown nodded her head in agreement.

Deaconess Brown placed both of her hands on the sides of my waist and pulled at my sweats, trying to get them off of me. Pastor Waters stopped her and inclined her face into my wet lap. She let out her tongue from in between her plum colored lips and twirled it up and down my dick print. Following the strokes of her tongue, she passionately kissed on my wet dick print. I tilted my head back and moaned,

"Ahhhhh shit — that feels so fucking good."

"Oops! Sorry for cussing Pastor," I quickly said, covering my mouth with my hand.

Pastor Waters raised her head from my lap and Deaconess Brown proceeded to take off my sweats. She grabbed hold of the side of my sweatpants, wiggling them down. I lifted my bottom from the edge, allowing her to pull them down to my ankles, and off the heels of my feet.

"In honor of successfully completing your baptism and being inducted into the holy crystal matrimony, we shall now bless your throne DJ," said Deaconess Brown.

Deaconess Brown took me into her hand and firmly clutched her fingers around my fully developed dick. I instantly tensed up, and then exhaled.

Pastor Waters inclined forward and swaddled her warm mouth on the head of my dick. Using only her spongy tongue and strong, moistened jaws, she slowly swallowed my dick head to the back of her wet mouth, locking her melting lips around the circumference of my dick.

Deaconess Brown slid her hand down to my swollen ball sack, massaging it, as Pastor Waters' head nodded up and down swiftly for minutes.

I started losing consciousness, moaning louder and louder in joyousness. I was being showered with satisfaction from the mouth and hand of two Heavenly Goddess servants, who were serving me — well.

My hardened dick was just fantasizing about thrusting the inner lining of their vaginas just moments earlier. Instead, he was thrusting the inner lining of the Pastor's jaws.

Deaconess Brown gradually inclined forward, connecting her lips with Pastor Waters' lips before letting her mouth slide back down my shaft. Their lips, tongues, and saliva intertwined on my dick, as I howled, "I'm about to cum; I'm about to cum."

Pastor Waters clenched the base of my dick very tightly with her fist, stopping my ejaculation and semen from shooting out the mouth of my dick.

I contracted my pelvic floor muscles briefly and my dick jerked, shooting a little sweet precum down the side of my throbbing dick. Deaconess Brown instantly licked it off, and Pastor Waters' tongue met with her tongue on the tip of my dick. They briefly wrestled their tongues for my precum.

French Vanilla Dick, I thought to myself.

Pastor Waters returned the favor for Deaconess Brown, supporting the base of my dick for her to climb on top of. Deaconess Brown quickly jumped out of the baptistery and on top of my lap, resting her hands on my shoulders. I cuffed and squeezed her golden round apple, as she pressed her small tinder lips hard onto mine. I sucked the cotton candy flavored lipstick right off the bottom of her lip. Deaconess Brown then took my bottom lip into her mouth and began suckling on it.

Pastor Waters then guided the head of my dick between the drizzling lips of Deaconess Brown. She slid me back and forth between them, pressing it firmly against her slippery, aroused clitoris.

Pastor Waters slowly inserted me deep into Deaconess Brown's tight, damped pussy, and released her firm grip.

I came instantly as Deaconess Brown slid her pussy down, swallowing my dick whole. I screamed in pleasure — blasting her walls and cervix with my powerful cum.

While I maintained my erection, Deaconess Brown immediately started straddling and pouncing her spongy pussy on my dick. She clenched her legs tightly around my lap, digging her fingernails into my shoulders. Within seconds, her strides intensified, as she cried loudly, releasing her milky cream all over my dick. Deaconess Brown's body fainted and she rested her head on my right shoulder.

Suddenly, I felt a hand pull me out of Deaconess Brown's creme-filled fountain.

I looked down, and it was Pastor Waters sliding me out. She inserted my creme-sickle into her mouth, suckling and slurping me loudly, devouring the blended flavors of Deaconess Brown and ME.

Milky Wet Galaxy

Jameel Davis

"BIG PURR"

Legs wide-open
Coupe
Switching gears
Riding shot-ty to the 6ix

Right hand, inner-thigh
Lace-thong
Fresh Brazilian
Fingers on her automatic-Start
Hellcat purring loud-ly

Creaming the-seats
Cruising the-streets
Driving her past city limits
Pussy Limits

Truck-Stop
Worry-Free
Fuck-N-Free
Duty Free
Her and Me

CN Tower
Pussy-Power
Pussy-Hour
Pussy-Purr

Big Purr
Pussy-cation
Ready?!

2
Chapter

"*Ready or Not, Here I Cum*"

"READY OR NOT, HERE I CUM"

I JUST WANT TO
SMILE
WHILE WATCHING
YOU CUM, WITHOUT
ME CUMING.
I'M ONLY HARD AND
DROOLING FOR YOU.

MAKE HER CUM

"MAKE HER CUM TOO"

Do Not Leave Until She Does!

She deserves to cum, all on your nose
Even if you can't Breathe.

"Ready or Not, Here I Cum"

81

Imma Satisfier— Satisfy-HER

Her Clitoris is my pacifier — imma pacifyHer.

"GOO GOO GAGA"

She allows me to suck on it often to keep me from crying — to keep me quiet, to keep me satisfied.

I am satisfied!

"Lay me on the floor, the couch or on your bed; hover your shiny pearl above me like a dangling crib toy and place you in my mouth."

Keep me quiet!

"Hush Big Daddy, don't you cry, Mama's going to sing you a lullaby — with your favorite Binky in your mouth."

"Rock-a-bye baby, on the tabletop, when your lips blow, my hips will rock…"

"Satisfy me — I need your satisfaction."

I am satisfied — that I satisfied her.
She knows imma satisfier — satisfy-Her, whenever I get to suck on her pacifier to pacifyHer.

"Ready or Not, Here I Cum"

Jameel Davis

Chanel No. 5 Paris

Date Night / Candle Light Dinner

Sexy Little Black Dress, Satin Embroidery Thong

(Wine) Cantina Castelnuovo Del Garda Prosecco Rosè!

Discipline by Janet Jackson

Scan & Listen

It's when she pulls her panties to the side, holds them in place, grabs my dick and slides it deep within her - for me.

JEALOUSY

I'm not jealous of anyone or anything, except her panties…

I am jealous of the fact they are more close to — and spend more time with — her than my mouth, fingers, and dick do.

I am jealous of the fact they have access to more of my favorite pineapple juice than my mouth, fingers, and dick do.

They just let it all go to waste.

I am jealous of the fact they have the luxury of sitting up under her everywhere she goes, and my mouth, fingers, and dick can't.

I am jealous of the fact she spends more money on them than me — and my mouth, fingers, and dick are the ones always making her drenched and happy.

I am jealous of the fact they are advertised on the 'gram more than me, and my mouth, fingers, and dick show her more appreciation than her followers.

I'm no longer peeling them off of her moistened lips and pulling them to the side when she wants me to hammer my dick inside her walls from the front, side, and back.

Instead, I'm going to rip them off, because they are always cock blocking, trying to slide back and stop me from making a mess.

86

"Ready or Not, Here I Cum"

Jameel Davis

YOU DESERVE DICK YOU CAN NUT ON

It's really a waste of time if you can't cum too
— All over his dick.

Just as bad as he want to nut up in you when you are squeezing your sponge-like walls around him

I know you are hungry to cum all over him.

It's very frustrating to you — and selfish of him to finish and you can't.

Bringing my woman to climax is one of the most rewarding experiences ever

And he is missing out on the greatest treatment ever, and so much of your craziness lol

For me, making my woman cum uncontrollably is the most exciting part about having sex.

If he can't return the favor, one you have done for him time and time again

Get him some help or cut him loose, so you can cum as crazy and as much as you want — all over some talented inches.

Granting the right lightening rod access inside of you, stroking your sponge-like walls with love until all of your muscles contract together, building up what you have been saving and releasing it on him as your body trembles — will bring pure happiness and satisfaction to your mind, body, and spirit.

You Deserve A Dick You Can Nut On.

Go and get that "Dick-cipline" you need.

Versace Yellow Diamonds

Celebration

Black Lace Panties, Purple Silk Robe

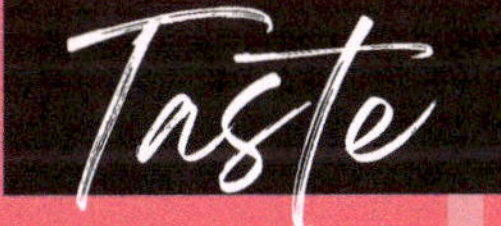

Dirty Martini, Pineapples

Diced Pineapples by Rick Ross ft. Wale & Drake

Scan & Listen

THE GRAND OPENING

"He fathered your children without you being able to nut all in his mouth, on his penis, and without your warm juices flowing down his balls as he promised you would? And he left you?"

"What A Selfish Dick!"

"An Unfulfilled Fantasy," I said.

Hey, hey; look at me, Keish!

"I know it's unfair and I am sorry that you couldn't celebrate the release of your pineapple juices with your friends during ladies' night," I said with concern.

"Keisha began to cry."

Hey, don't cry. It's ok!

"I'll throw you a ribbon-cutting ceremony and we can cut that red bow right off of those Black Lace Vicky Panties together and give you a proper grand opening," I said, attempting to break the ice to make her feel better.

"Every woman needs to experience an orgasm and I know you could use one…or a few. It will turn your world around and make you feel so much better as a woman."

"Wait! How do you know what kind of panties I have on?" Keisha responded with a surprised look on her face. "And how are you so sure you can make me have one?"

"When you stretched your torso, your shirt rolled up and revealed the red bow on the top of your panties."

"Keisha, I am a man of action, and there is only one way to find out how sure I am. No pressure! But if you really would like to experience what many other women are experiencing on a regular basis, I say take me up on my offer."

"And what if you don't deliver?" Keisha shot back.

"Not only am I a man of action, but I am also a man of integrity. I deliver on my word and I am versed on the female anatomy and reproductive system. It's second nature. My aim is to please woman; it's my nature," I said with extreme confidence.

"Look, put his kids in bed— I mean your kids — and meet me in the kitchen over by the stove."

I took a moment to think to myself after admiring how beautiful Keisha looked despite having multiple children.

Wow, Keish looks so goooood. I can't even tell she gave birth to three beautiful children!

I could only imagine how beautiful her pussy looked and how good it would feel to have her clitoris gliding back and forth on my soft wet mouth until her warm frosting stained my tongue.

I bet she has her pussy trimmed fine and shaped like the top of a martini glass.

"Oooh, a Dirty Martini with Pineapple on the Rocks."

"Hey Keish, I am excited to see you have come to take me up on my offer. Please, allow me to help you take a seat on the counter by the butter rolls. I have a craving for something sweet: your tropical treat beneath that purple silk robe," I said flirtatiously.

"A Purple Robe?"

Wait! Does she know that's my favorite color?

"Holy Goddess Spirit of Pussy take me to her Fountain of Youth; she can dip and bathe my whole face in her life-giving water!" Once I get going, drinking from her Spring, I ain't stopping until I am full and her well has run dry."

"Keisha, suckle on my bottom lip if you grant me permission to take full control of this ceremony and permission to turn on your cell phone camera and record this groundbreaking moment."

"Instead of sharing a story neither of your friends are going to believe, I want you to show them this video of you celebrating the grand release of your pineapple juices all over me."

"Hello Keisha. Welcome to the Grand Opening and Ribbon Cutting Ceremony for your Pineapple Juice Bar.

Before I indulge you and begin my liquid fast, allow me to bless you — and the main ingredient in the smoothie that has been prepared for me — and express my silent gratitude to my personal savior for this opportunity."

Dear Pineapple,

Bless Me, oh Bless Me with your vitamins and nutrients which I am about to receive from your roots, which will soon be blasted down my esophagus. I apologize for you not being cared for, kissed on, licked on, sucked on, swallowed, and digested properly.

"Thank you Heavenly Goddess Spirit of Pussy for not granting her kids father's weak, selfish mouth and dick the ability to bring her extreme sexual pleasure, and for granting me the opportunity to be the first to create fireworks inside of her beautiful melanated body right here in her kitchen. I'm about to give Kiesha the best sex of her life and her friends are about to be jealous-jealous after watching this groundbreaking experience."

Oh Dear Pineapple, you will soon be able to produce gallons of your juice after my tongue begins to vibrate on your juicy flesh.

Thank you for your love and flavor. Bless my tongue and this countertop we pray, Awomen!"

"Hey Keish, relax for a second; I gotta grab you a bib. I know she's about to be spitting up soon," I said, bursting into laughter.

Keisha, watch me closely, as I begin to slowly separate your trembling thighs from each other and peel off your drenched panties from your pretty, warm, damped vagina.

"Damn, she's so wet!" I said to myself. She's leaking through these Black Lace Vicky Panties and the tips of my fingers are very moist just from touching them."

"I can't wait to suck her juices all off of my fingertips just to see how she reacts."

"Oooh, she's spitting up! Look at it race down her thighs!"

These gold plated ribbon-cutting scissors are for us to cut the ribbon. Remember, this red one holding these together?"

You take the right side, and I'll take the left.

On your count of three, I will cut the ribbon, we will smile for your camera and open the doors to your juice bar. Get ready for me to give you the satisfaction you deserve.

"One two…"

"Before she said three, her Vicky panties were already off and my mouth was planted right on her fountain. 'Lap Lap Lap Lap Lap Lap Lap Lap Lap Lap Lap Lap Lap Lap.' There was no need for me to smile for the camera, when her pussy lips already had me blushing."

"Damn! Casper let all of this go to waste…

"Ladies night is tomorrow night, right?" I asked Keisha with a pleasant smile.

"Yeah it is, but I didn't plan on going. I was hoping y'all was up for another round of battle of the sexes. She and I versus you and him again," Keisha grinned, nodding her head at my dick print she saw nudging through my boxer briefs.

"We have plenty of time for that. Go on, enjoy yourself, and celebrate with your friends. It's your time to shine. You can tell me about it later, I encouraged Keisha.

"Hey y'all, I think my kids may have a new step-daddy."

"What? When? How?

"I finally got my kitty tamed last night and this beautiful man hit all of my spots with his mouth and with his dick after I confessed to him about never having an orgasm before."

"Ooo, this is juicy. Let me grab my wine."

"Continue."

"Girl, I'm surprised this man's mouth isn't numb and he ain't dead yet from volunteering to let me waterboard him. My kid's daddy has never eaten my pussy that good. I came all over my kitchen counter and his freaky ass slurped it all up like an ICEE."

"Tell me more."

"And his dick. My goodness, It's Amazing! "It's magical! I kissed, licked, and sucked all on it, just for making me cum sooo many times. After he came, he started fucking me again. Then he came again and started fucking me again. I had to kick his ass off me."

"I have never heard of— or met — a man who can cum back to back, to back. I thought y'all said only women can do that and when a man cum, that's it?"

"Shut your lying, no good dick getting ass up Keisha. Out of the blue your ass pops up with a man with a golden dick?

Bullshit!"

"Oh yeah?! Y'all wanna see?"

Aroma

(Male) Prada by Luna Rosa, (Female) Donna Born In Roma Valentino

Mood

Special Delivery

Sight

(Male) Trojan Fire & Ice, Gray Cotton Shorts, White T-shirt, Gray & White Tennis Shoes, (Female) His Black T-shirt & Your Panties

Taste

Tequila and Lime Juice

Sound

Yo Body by Ann Marie

Scan & Listen

HYPER-SA-LI-VATION

There's no pussy better than a pussy that has already climaxed Before her panties came off.

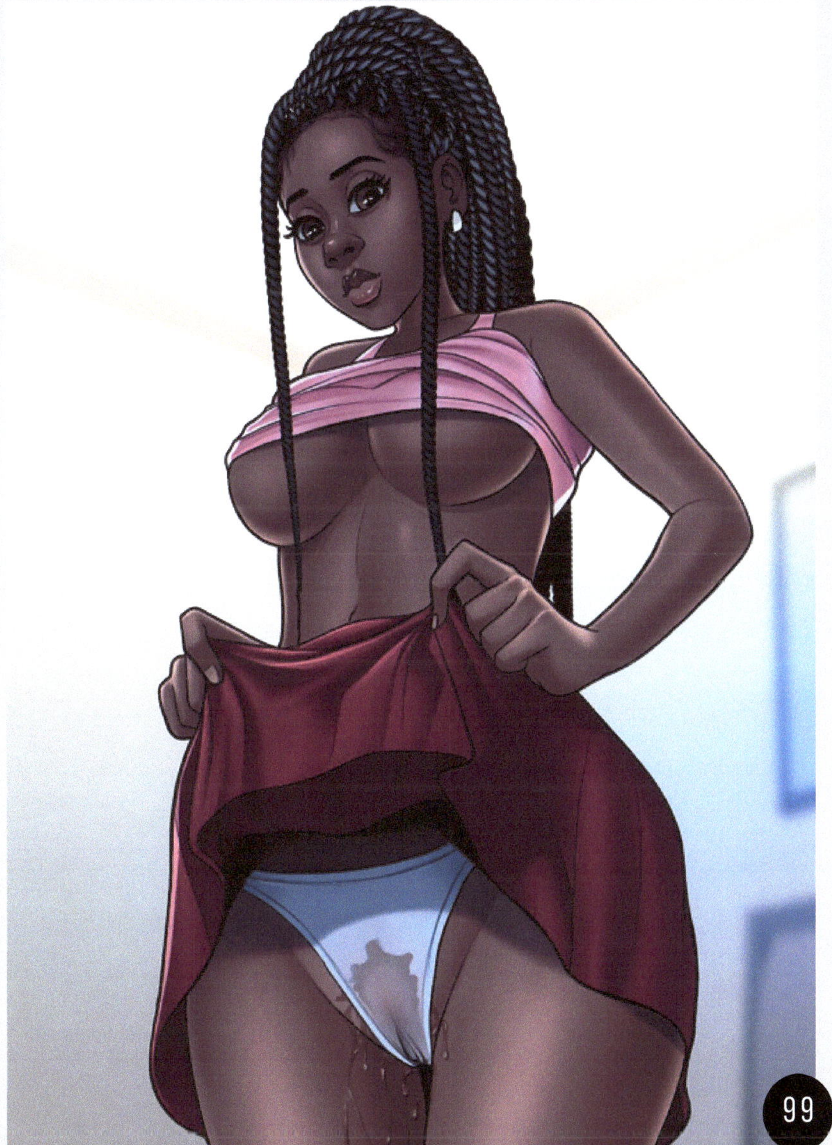

It's been months since I first jumped off the Diving Board — entering head first inside of her deep kinetic waters below. When I first made contact with her waters, I created the biggest splash ever, immediately cooling off both of our warm bodies. I remember slowly swimming back to the surface and began treading her waters, making her cum over and over again — all over me.

Bobbing in her tasty waters and rafting her white water rapids was such a wild adventure.

Still reminiscing about our first extreme water adventure, Alesha has been begging me nonstop for a game of Water Pogo off into her deep-end.

Today is Giving Tuesday, her lifeguards are off duty, and I have made arrangements to surprise her with a special dick-livery wrapped in Fire & Ice for added passion and thrilling sensations of pleasure — for a round of Water Pogo in her splash park.

It's after 9 o'clock and I just pulled up to the entrance of her condo. I was showered in Midnight body wash and cologne from Bath & Body Works. I wore my gray cotton shorts that revealed my dick print, and a white t-shirt with some gray and white tennis shoes. I came ready to stroke and splash away in her deep-end.

"Ready or Not, Here I Cum"

Jameel Davis

I bypassed and greeted a tall, medium build, brown-skinned male wearing dreads with a head nod, who was exiting the condo door that led to Alesha's suite. The door was closing fast behind him and I wanted to catch it before it locked. I didn't want to spoil the surprise dick-livery by having to call her to let me inside. Being careful not to spill my solo red cup filled with tequila and lime juice, I moved as quickly as I could, and slid between the unattended door before it shut. Once I was inside, I crept up the three short flights of stairs that led up to her condo door. I knocked on her door loud enough to be undetected by her nearby neighbors and security officers.

Alesha opened the door wearing a pink tank top shirt that hugged her B-cup breasts. She wore a red tennis skirt that traced her thick brown thighs and luscious ass. She extended her neck all the way back to see who I was and instantly clinched her legs together, melting in her panties with excitement.

Alesha led me inside and secured the door behind us. Once inside, I removed my tennis shoes at the door and made my way into her living room, then into her kitchen to wash my hands. After drying my hands, I sat on top of her marble countertop, and sipped on my tequila and lime until she returned from the nearby washroom.

Alesha returned from the washroom bottomless, wearing just her t-shirt. Alesha sexy-walked-on-over to where I was sitting, stood between my legs, and rested her hands on my upper thighs. She then slid her hands beneath my shorts and began rubbing them up and down my thighs. Alesha then leaned in and started kissing on the right side of my neck. While her lips trailed my neck line, I reached my right arm around her and cuffed the bottom of her left ass cheek. My hand quickly slid off her wet ass cheek that got wet from a silent orgasm she released just from embracing me.

I moved my hand from around her, retrieved the Fire & Ice wrapper from my pocket, sat it on the counter, and eased three of my fingers between her slithery kissing thighs. Once I reached her squirting clitoris, she stood erect, squatted, and moaned quietly, as I cuddled and caressed her clitoris in circular motions — washing my hand in ounces of her pleasure. Anxious to wrap her thirsty mouth around my growing dick, Alesha quickly retrieved my dick from my boxers and took off my gray cotton shorts and underwear. She then kneeled down and took an inch and a half of my dick into her narrow mouth. Realizing she had bitten off way more than she could chew, she took me out of her mouth and laid down onto the kitchen floor. She reached for my hands, signaling me to join her on the floor to insert my raft into her wild rapids. I retrieved the Fire & Ice protective covering from beside me on the counter and instructed her to get up and put it on me.

"Ready or Not, Here I Cum"

Jameel Davis

Alesha stood up, tore open the covering, and rolled it all the way down my enlarged dick. She anticipated me following her back down to the floor, instead I signaled for her to climb her short sexy ass up on the countertop and sit on my dick.

Alesha climbed up onto the marble countertop, held onto my shoulders with her hands, and threw her right thigh across my lap. As her leg came across me, her aqua jetted out from her oozing lips and onto my lap. My dick was rock solid; she had me horny as fuck. Alesha lifted her luscious ass and I emerged my hardened dick deep inside of her warm, slippery, and snuggled pussy. After settling my muscles when I got all the way inside of her, Alesha contracted her pussy muscles around me, and took on my raft with her fierce white currents. The Fire & Ice shot cool thrilling sensations deep into her vagina, and she galloped on my dick cowgirl style as if she was on the back of an untamed stallion. Within minutes, she squeezed her arms around my neck and cried with rapture, as she released her tsunami all over the both of us, and down onto the countertop. The pressure from her tidal wave sent warm thrilling sensations back to my throbbing dick and she increased her speed at the sound of I'm Cumming. Alesha gripped my dick tighter and tighter with her gushing walls as she rode me — releasing another wave all over us.

"Ready or Not, Here I Cum"

Jameel Davis

My penile dorsal vein throbbed hard on her G-spot — as I filled the inner lining of the rain jacket with large amounts of my warm icing, that ejected from the mouth of my dick.

I sighed with bliss and Alesha hopped down from the marble countertop and handed me my bottoms. She escorted me to the front door of her condo, stopped, and dropped to her knees. She pulled my dick back out of my boxers and put what she could fit in her mouth — and she sucked him goodbye.

Water Pogo!

"*Ready or Not, Here I Cum*"

Jameel Davis

PASTA FOR PUMA

"Ready or Not, Here I Cum"

Trade your Puma places with his Pasta Noodles

Let him Slurp You Up as you scoot back and forth on his tongue till you erupt,

Slowly drizzling his favorite icing all down his esophagus.

Ahhhh!

Jameel Davis

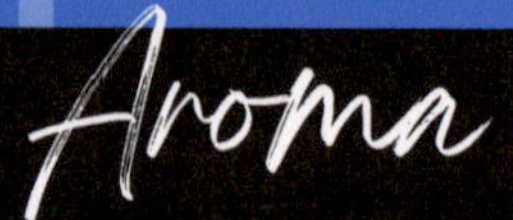

Gucci Guilty by Gucci

First Encounter

Blazer, V-Neck, Jeans, Casual Shoes, Watch

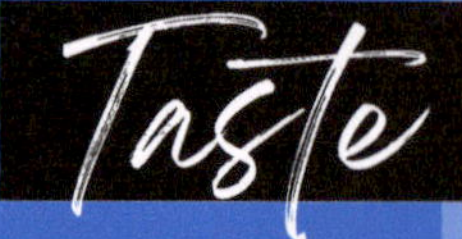

Woodford Reserve

That's What It's Made For
by Usher

Scan & Listen

THAT'S WHAT IT'S MADE FOR

Figured I'd come and get a sip of that pussy one night,
And if you allow me, and it's sweet to me,
I'll tongue kiss it and slurp it all night.

I can picture warm sweet nectar trickling down ya thighs,

I know you want it,
I promise you will nut up,
When you nut up, I'll lick it up,
Don't be shy.

Guess your moans have been too low,
Time to turn them up loud.
Scared to put my whole face in it,
Just ain't my style.

I wanna play in the puddles,
As I hear you moaning loud,
You got what I'm craving for,

My tongue, you should be squirting on it.

You're right!
Come on and get it!

"Ready or Not, Here I Cum"

Jameel Davis

That's what it's made for!

This pussy ready daddy!

That's what it's made for!

But, you gotta let me turn around!

You Know I Got It!
And imma make you cum like this….

Stay where you are,
That's what it's made for!

Imma Lick it, lick it, lick it down,
That's what it's made for!

Don't you turn around,
I got it!

Imma make you come like this…

So I can eat it up like this baby,
Slide my whole tongue in it like this baby,

*No more frowning,
Imma make that pussy smile like this :-)*

"Ready or Not, Here I Cum"

Jameel Davis

Acqua di Gioia by Giorgio Armani

Mood

Happy Hour

Sight

High Waisted Skinny Jeans, Crisp White T-shirt,
Fitted Blazer, Heeled Sandals

Taste

Classic Margarita

Sound

Scan & Listen

SUFFOCATE

Greetings from above,

Had she worn one of those sundresses I like instead of those denim jeans

And nothing else to cover you

I'd crawl beneath this table and plant my thirsty mouth on you

Licking and sucking all over you (just the way you like it) with joy until the waitress returns with our meal.

What was the point of her getting a Brazilian Wax and freshening you up — just to suffocate you?

Knowing she's going to eventually want to sit and twirl you all on my face until you shower me with pleasure.

Now I have to wait for you to suck on my tongue (how I like it), when I could have just placed my tongue inside you right now.

I know it's hard for you to breathe inside there, but I only ordered an appetizer. I want you as my entree. So, we won't be here long.

In the event you begin to faint and pass out on the way home, I'll pull the car over and give you mouth to mouth until you foam at the mouth and she screams in satisfaction.

"Ready or Not, Here I Cum"

Jameel Davis

excellence flows freely
through my mouth like the
Nile River.

"Ready or Not, Here I Cum"   Jameel Davis

Versace Eros

Sprung

Fresh Haircut (Shadow Fade), Black Hanes Boxer Briefs, Black A-shirt

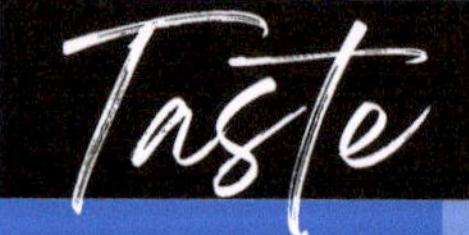

Warm Apple Cider with Fresh Cut Apples, Nutmeg and Whiskey

I'm Sprung by T-Pain

Scan & Listen

CREAM-SICLE

I love it when you cum all in your panties while you suck on this dick.

And when you cum immediately after inserting the tip of it between your drooling twin lips — sliding all inches deep into the mouth of your pussy.

Cumming...again

You got me wrapped around your — pussy

I Love You!

"Ready or Not, Here I Cum"   Jameel Davis

BACKWASH.

Can you just dab a bit of it on my tongue?
I want to sample it before overindulging.

I thought about sealing the pages in this book with a kiss of your clear, sweet, sticky liquid —juice you want me to help you produce from my pink lips. Those you have been craving to whine and press your clit up against.

But, I had a change of heart.

Instead, I was thinking you could kiss me, and stain my tongue with your delicious juices after you finish slurping you all off of my dick, and putting your tasty tongue back in my mouth.

Ahhhh!

"Ready or Not, Here I Cum"

Jameel Davis

"Ready or Not, Here I Cum"

Jameel Davis

Chapter 3

"Gag & Go"

"GAG & GO"

SUCK HIS DICK - WITH LOVE & PASSION

When you start to gag, it doesn't mean quit.

It means, wipe away your tears and gag on it until your soft palate is accustomed to being touched by the head of his swollen dick — gradually touch it until you are comfortable with it digging deeper and deeper into the back of your throat.

So what if you cry — that's what you asked for.

"Gag & Go"

Jameel Davis

Miss Dior Blooming Bouquet by Dior

Classy But Nasty

French Mani & Pedi, Natural Kinky Hair Tied In A Messy Bun, Men's T-shirt, Micro Thongs, Laptop and Book

A Grapefruit & Orange Juice

Morning by Teyana Taylor

Scan & Listen

HIGHER HEAD

Sometimes I wonder if I am the only man who feels like I am *"The Man"* when my soul is getting snatched at the mercy of my elegant and sophisticated Black Woman.

 Each time, I feel as if I am sitting on the highest throne with the world's most amazing species, with the softest, wettest, and juiciest mouth wrapped around me.

It's something very, very special about *my educated Black Woman kneeling before me, trying her very best to suck the smooth melanated skin right off my long, thick, and curved, caramel skinned dick, in the most nastiest, sexiest, pleasurable, and educated way.*

"Guy & Go"

Jameel Davis

Nothing else in the world matters during that moment.

My charming Black Woman gets cute for the dick: hair, nails and feet. She even cooks for the dick, and buys fruit for the dick. And I don't even like grapefruit.
She wraps her hair, curls up right beside and takes naps with the dick — wakes up and puts her mouth backwards on the dick, at 5:00 A.M.

This intelligent Black gem has this dick shining operation down to a science, forming just the right amount of saliva in her mouth as if her taste buds have been anticipating my arrival and the taste of me, and creating the perfect "O" shape with her plump, glossy lips prior to my entry.

It's like she has studied the entire anatomy and physiology of the penis — at its resting and erect state — her entire life. She knows what to do to wake him up, keep him firm, and to put him right back to sleep, like a newborn baby.

She knows how to caress and hold him with the right amount of firmness and care, with her gel-polished nails, ensuring I don't slip away from her.

That continuous two-handed up and downward twist and neck roll motion, she does as she slurps, licks, sucks, and spits on the dick until I cum uncontrollably is a feeling to die for. I almost died before, because after I climaxed, the only thing she stopped doing was spitting. That continuous two-handed up and downward twist and neck roll motion, as she slurps, licks, and sucks the head of my dick continues until she squeezes and sucks the last drop of sweet nut out of me with excitement, or until I beg for mercy for her to let it go.

"Gag & Go"

Jameel Davis

Did you receive your Master's in "<u>HIGHER H.E.A.D</u>. (Harmonizing an Erect, Advanced Dick)?"

Who taught you that?

It's the most beautiful and rewarding sight ever, to look in the eyes of the world's most amazing species — my Black elegant, sophisticated woman — as she snatches the spirit right out of my body with her hands and mouth, and smiles as she makes a mess all in her panties.

I LOVE WHEN YOU SUCK DADDY DICK

I Love the feeling of my Big Dick sliding hands-free across the top of your tongue, across the roof of your mouth, to the back of your tongue, around your tonsils, as you gag on it, allowing it to penetrate back and forth down your throat.

I Love it when you pop him right out of my boxer-briefs in mid-day and your eyes light up with excitement at the sight of him — putting your wet lips, tongue, and jaws right to work — stretching him to his maximum reach and firmness.

I Love when you drive this boat.

I Love when you gradually place the head gently on your soft palate, voluntarily making yourself produce tears — sobbing and slobbering all over on my dick.

I Love when I slide your loose hair away from your face, gripping your hair into a bun — guiding your head back and forth, as you swallow my dick freely without interruption.

I Love when you open your mouth and stick your tongue out in a thirstful manner — squeezing and blasting the first shot of my sweet cream down the back of your mouth and massaging the rest out on your tongue — digesting the contents with satisfaction.

"Gag & Go"   _Jameel Davis_

VENOM

"Her saliva was like butter; I damn near nutted all in her mouth within seconds of her sucking on the head of her dick like a lemon drop, making it disappear into her mouth."

To prevent Symone aka "Suction Cup" from overpowering this talented dick of mine, I contracted my pelvic floor muscles (a skill I developed when the urge to bust comes too soon) giving me extra momentum to last longer in her buttery mouth. I do this when her mouth is just too watery and her jaws are too damn powerful for me to last naturally. There have been a couple times where Symone sucked me dry as soon as she took me in —I couldn't even develop the thought to hold it back. She has her moments where she goes for the kill— which is usually after I bring her wild, intense waves of pleasure that begin deep inside and radiate through the rest of her body — causing her to shudder as she cum all on my dick and mouth.

On this particular night, ending an adventurous weekend, I knew Symone was up to no good and was out to get my ass back after I latched onto her, and was smacking on her pearl-like clitoris with my tongue and lips all weekend long — extracting her sticky clear fluids from her body. I did this all while licking my come-finger and fuck-finger as they simultanously penetrated her G-spot and A-spot in a come-hither motion. And, as she was nutting something crazy all over my lips and trying her best to keep from being heard, her rectum contracted — sucking my fuck-finger in and out of her anus, coating my finger with a jelly-like substance. That moment was magical, I had Symone's body at my leisure, and it was beautiful watching her body go through the motions. Seconds after slowly pulling my slimy fingers out of her body and lifting my Cobra tongue from her sensitive clitoris, she was sound asleep.

"I want some milk from your dick before I go," Symone demanded.

As I secured the door to my bedroom, Symone jumped up and down, and moaned with excitement as I pulled my pants down to reveal the Mealticket she anxiously wanted to put her buttery mouth all over. I sat on the love seat near where she stood and she dropped onto her knees, crawled over, and buried her face right in my lap. Symone held the shaft of my semi-erect dick, submerged it into her watery mouth, and locked her powerful jaws around it. I was ready to cum before I was fully swollen inside of her venomous mouth. But, I wasn't ready; I couldn't let her do me like she did those other times. So, I contracted my pelvic floor muscles and gave myself an extra four minutes as she attacked my dick like a Spitting-Cobra.

Because of how increasingly fast and hard she was swallowing my dick, I was barely able to maintain my posture and composure on the love seat. I eventually fell over, leaning to my right side and Symone shifted her body with me, working her mouth and neck on my dick from the side. Symone's round ass was within arms reach; I sucked on my fuck-finger then slid it down her pants and worked it inside of her ass. Once I was inside of her, my finger found the spot (A-spot) that made her go "oooh" and she started wagging her tail as she sucked my dick harder and faster, releasing more of her venom. That turned me on even more. I was ready to cum.

I moaned loud enough for Symone to hear me, "I'm bout to-cum so-good." As she increased the speed of her mouth on my dick at the sound of my words, she spit more of her venom on it— as I pressed my finger pad repeatedly against her button as if I was ringing a doorbell — increasing my pressure and speed until I filled her mouth up with all of me.

After Symone squeezed the last drop of cum into her mouth, she continued sucking the life out of me, paralyzing my entire body and immediately sending me into an eleven hour coma.

Symone went from being called "Suction Cup" to "Venom," and I've been scared of the Buttery Queen Cobra Head ever since.

"Gag & Go"   _Jameel Davis_

SPOTLIGHT

It is very rude of you to stop swallowing your dick while in the company of others.

That is your dick — continue to make it disappear until it cum deep into your mouth.

"*Gag & Go*"

Jameel Davis

What are you ashamed of?

I eat that pussy effortlessly regardless of who's
around, don't I?

Let the onlookers see how much you love spit-
shining and making love to me with your warm
mouth.

Even the people in blue.

When they shine their flashlight into the window of
the car in the parking lot of your church or pull out
their camera phone to record us for evidence, that is
your moment of glory.

That is your spotlight — Don't choke.

Get your shine on and go crazy with your wet
mouth.

Sound off and suck it fast —spit shining your dick
with your thick saliva.

Slurp it up and down, and gag on it — baptizing
daddy dick deeper into your throat until you are
pulled out of the car and placed in cuffs.

Earn your citation with pride and stand in front of
the judge licking your lips with a smile.

That a girl!

"Gag & Go"   Jameel Davis

STANDING OVATION

> If you aren't using it to sing, why is your
> hand all on my mic?
> Put it down if you aren't performing
> tonight.
>
> This here-mic is for that special female
> artist with wind, a wet mouth, and who
> is ready to blow the color right off of it
> — in record-breaking intervals.

Hello, I would like to welcome you to Brain Freeze — I go by the name, *"Tap Out,"* and I'll be your host tonight.

Our featured guest *"SJ"* strives again to conquer the most well-equipped microphone, on the hottest stage on the planet and as always, I am striving to make her Tap Out.

Placing her right hand firmly around the shaft of my golden mic, removing it from its holder — *SJ* guides her melting mouth towards it, introducing her lips to the head.

Jameel Davis

Hello...

SJ took me inside her winterfresh mouth for nearly 11 minutes, singing with all of her might, eager to extract the creamy contents from its tube. Contents she had anticipated on retrieving 10 minutes and 30 seconds ago with her cool and hot tactic. Her knees, tonsils, and jawline grew weak after 10 minutes of trying to make me erupt like a volcano. SJ was confident that she could break the record for peeling my top back and making me cum within seconds.

I had to remind our featured guest, top peeled back or not, this dick runs forever — naturally.

I finally decided to stop withholding my creamy contents from SJ, when I felt her mouth grow tired — losing her grip.

I retrieved my golden mic from SJ's hand as she pressed her soft-round ass on the seat of the nearby stool. I stood over her and held my mic near her mouth. She stretched open her soft lips and quickly placed two small cubes of ice on the center of her smooth tongue — before feeling my thick, warm shots of vanilla cream plunge into the back of her mouth.

"Ice Ice Ba-by."

Standing Ovation!

Chapter 4

"Two Can Play that Game"

"TWO CAN PLAY THAT GAME"

(Male) Givenchy Paris, (Female) Mon Paris by Yves Saint Laurent

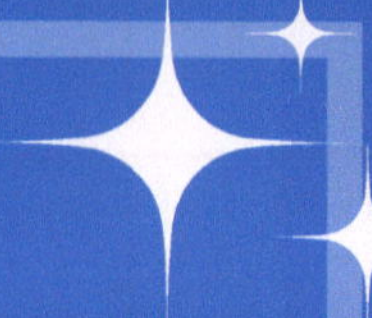

Mood

Desperate

Sight

(Female) Mini Sundress, Buckle Strap Heels, Pink Lace Thongs, (Female) Ponytail, Mini White High Waisted Button Front Pencil Skirt, Soft Blush Pink Top, Light Pink Vinyl Ankle Strap Heel Sandals, Pink and White BALENCIAGA Top Handle Satchel Bag, Johnson's Baby Oil, (Male) Red Tie, White Dress Shirt, Red Stacey Adams shoes, Black Slacks, Black Boxers

Taste

Coffee, Pastries, Hennessy

Sound

You Remind Me of Something by R. Kelly

Scan & Listen

TEST DRIVE

Tash wasn't even thinking about this dick until her friend Diamond told her all about this V8 Supercharged Dick with the Hemi she fell in love with after she test drove it around the block a couple times.

"Hey Gurl, guess what?" Diamond asked with excitement. "What Gurl?" Tash asked. I met this fine-ass guy named Jay, he's a dicksman — I mean a salesman— on the automile. You know my income taxes just hit my account and I took a Lyft to his lot to look for a new ride. After I got there, he showed me around and then showed me his dick, and it was so fucking beautiful. I have never seen a dick so fine in my life."

"Diamond, are you serious?" asked Tash.

"Hell the fuck yeah, I'm serious." His dick was thick and long, and had a sparkling peanut butter coat with not one scratch on it. Gurl, you know how much I love anything with peanut butter! His dick looked so damn good and I could tell it had low miles on it. My mouth watered, staring at it. I wanted to lick the peanut butter all off his fine-ass dick.

"Two Can Play that Game"   *Jameel Davis*

"Okay, tell me more. Did you touch it? What did it feel like? Did he let you taste it?" Tash asked anxiously.

"Tash, Jay saw how fascinated I was about his dick and asked if I wanted to test drive it around the block. It's like he already knew what I was thinking. And, you know my scary, clumsy ass didn't want to go anywhere near it at first. I didn't want to fuck up nothing I could not pay for. He told me to follow him as he headed to the back showroom. Remind you Tash, the dealership had already closed and everyone except Jay and I had already left for the evening. I wanted him so bad, but was scared someone would come back in and catch us."

"So you fucked him? Was the dick good?" asked Tash.

"Gurl, let me finish telling you the story, damn," Diamond demanded.

"So look, I followed him to the back showroom and I was nervous as fuck, but my pussy was excited at the same damn time. I really wanted to test drive his dick before I left and headed back home. I haven't had no dick in months and I damn sure wasn't tryna to fuck Tommy quick pipper ass again. I needed something new and long lasting that I could grip this tight-ass pussy around and cum all over. She's been hungry for some dick with a thick middle vein that could massage her gums and make her cum again and again.

"Two Can Play that Game"   *Jameel Davis*

I didn't want to just give her to anybody; he had to be worth this bomb-ass pussy. Jay's big sexy dick was the one I wanted to dump this big ole ass on right there in the dealership. Everything about him just made me want to give him some: he was gentle, smelled nice, handsome, and was about his business. But still, I was nervous as fuck."

"Umm hmm. So what did you have on? Something easy and accessible, I know," Tash said, answering herself.

"I wore a blue, sultry ruched mini sundress, with some neon buckle-strapped heels, with a pair of my favorite pink lace thongs I got from Wet Seal. Each step I took following behind Jay, my dress rose up and my pussy got wetter and wetter, leaking over my thong, and down my inner thighs."

"Gurl, this is some juicy shit! I can't believe my ears," said Tash in an excited tone.

"Once we reached the showroom, Jay untied his red tie, took off his white dress shirt, kicked off his red Stacy Adams shoes, took off his black slacks and boxers — and laid on top of the desk in his office. That thick, long, shiny peanut butter dick was standing there at full attention, waiting for me to climb up and sit this tight pussy on top of it.

"Two Can Play that Game"   _Jameel Davis_

I tried squeezing my legs together to stop my pussy from throbbing, instead, I squeezed out more of my pussy juices, trickling it down my thighs."

"My pussy is getting wet from listening to you, Diamond. Hurry up so I can get off this phone and call Mr. Man to come plug this leak," lied Tash.

"Jay looked over at me and noticed me trying to hold back the river that was flowing beneath my mini dress. He was so damn cocky, Tash. He said to me, grinning, "why waste it all on your thighs, when you could be letting it flow all down this big dick I have prepared for you? I know you want it; I can tell how your body is reacting to the sight of it. Come over here and have a seat on it."

"Damn, Diamond. He wasn't trying to waste no time! Sounds like he knew what to do with that thang," Tash said, laughing.

"My knees grew nervous at the sound of his words, and I shivered. I walked slowly on over to where he was lying after he signaled for me to come on over. My pussy wanted him bad as fuck, but my mind was so scared. When I reached the desk, he took one of his fingers and wiped up the juice that dripped from my pussy onto my thigh and sucked it off of his finger.

"Two Can Play that Game"   *Jameel Davis*

Tash, I damn near melted all over the dealership floor."

"He's nasty," Tash giggled.

"I know right? Jay grabbed my hand and helped pull me up on the desk — on top of him. Instead of trying to quickly put that thick muthafucka right in my pussy, he grabbed me by my ass and lifted me up towards his face. I scooted up and he slid my thong to the side, licked up the remaining juices from my thighs, and put his tongue right inside my pussy — up to my G-spot. Tash, his mouth made me lose control and I fucked the shit out his nose. I cried a river all over his face."

"Damn, you put a Diamond on his tongue and he ate it good? Gurl don't tell me that's the only good thing that happened. What else did he do?" Tash asked curiously.

"After eating my pussy— letting me make a mess all over his face and desk —he reached into the desk drawer, pulled out a golden wrapper — tore it open and slowly rolled it down his long dick. You know he didn't even let me lick the peanut butter off of his dick like I wanted to?"

"What, you didn't taste the dick? Gurl, you crazy. I would have snatched that condom off and sucked the skin of his dick," Tash said with a surprised look on her face.

"I know yo freaky ass would have," Diamond smiled. I guess he didn't want me to smear his fresh peanut butter paint job," Diamond giggled.

"Once the condom was on, Jay grabbed me by my ass and pulled me back down near his dick. He held onto this ass with one hand, while holding my pink thong in place to the side. He used his other hand to slide the head of his dick right into this tight juicy pu-na-ny. I don't know if his dick was just that big, or if my pussy was just that tight from not fucking for all those months! Either way, Jay cranked his Supercharged Hemi Dick deep inside of me, and I took that powerful muthafucka for a spin, Tash. He went from zero to sixty in six seconds, pounding the fuck out of this pussy like I had missed a payment or something. Jay fucked me so damn good, I thought we were going to break his desk."

"I just know you threw that pussy back on his ass, don't tell me you tapped-out— not my best-friend," Tash wondered.

"Tash you know damn well, this pussy got some fire power. It may have been parked in the garage for months, but this pussy still got some work. I threw this pussy back on his dick — it backfired on the dick, each time he rushed it inside of me," Diamond laughed. "Gurl, Jay's thick, long dick was nothing like I had ever rode before. He has the smoothest and most powerful dick I have ever taken on. Jay's dick is fully loaded with horsepower and it has a manual transmission.

"Two Can Play that Game"

Jameel Davis

I took this pussy on a whole ass adventure. I kicked it in whichever gear I wanted, neutral, first, second, third, and fourth during my test drive, and I can't tell you how many times he made me cum all on his gear stick. Jay fucked me a brand new pussy — my body felt wonderful."

"I didn't want to leave, but I knew I had to go because the shop had already closed. I fixed my hair, handed him my thongs for keepsake, pulled down my dress, gave him a smile — dropped my deposit, and wobbled my ass on up out of that shop. Tash, that was the best day of my fucking life, and fuck needing another test drive, I'm going back to drive the bad boy right off the lot! Along with the car I came for."

"I don't think I ever had a man do some kinky shit like that before. I mean, I had some good dick before, but nothing that made me want to buy it," Tash envied.

"Yeah, well you are missing out," Diamond replied.

"Diamond, you out here advertising dick that ain't yours, for someone like me to suck and fuck, and make mine. I'll make his dick smile when he sees me," Tash said confidently with a laugh.

"Two Can Play that Game"

Jameel Davis

"Your desperate ass better not go up there and try to take my car either. I know how you are," Diamond demanded. I've been wanting a sports car for the longest and that's the only rare V8 sports car on the lot. That peanut butter Hemi is all mine, and he knows it. He's holding it in the garage for me and I will bring the rest of my balance on Monday when I get off work," Diamond exclaimed.

"Gurl, I'm just joking. I'm not going to try and fuck Jay with the Peanut Butter Dick— that's your Mr. Lover Man," Tash lied, laughing.

"Yeah, right! Don't you try no slick shit either," Diamond laughed.

"Look gurl, I gotta get going. I just wanted to tell you I let the cat out of the bag and rode it on some bomb-ass dick, attached to a bomb-ass man. I'm going to call you later, okay?" Diamond said with excitement.

"Okay gurl; I'll talk to you later."

It was only a matter of time before Tash became greedy and went after this V8 Supercharged Dick with the Hemi, she could not afford.

Monday afternoon had arrived and Tash was on her mission.

"Hello, thank you for calling Jay's Classic Sports Ride. How may I direct your call?"

"Hello and good afternoon, my name is Tash. Am I speaking with Jay the dickman, I mean the manual transmission specialist?"

"Yes, this is me," Jay chuckled.

"Great. Jay, I heard your ad on the Auto Trader radio commercial for a six second, manual transmission, peanut butter sports car with Melanin Muscle. I was wondering if you still had the car available?"

"Yes, I still have the car here, however, it's being held for a customer who already put down her deposit to secure the car. In fact, she's supposed to come in today to pay the remaining balance and take it home with her."

"Fuck! I really wanted that car. Is that the only one you have?"

"Unfortunately yes, it's the only one I have. It's a very rare and valuable vehicle and the only one of its kind in the world."

"Damn! Jay, by any chance I'm able to stop in to take a quick look at it and pose for pictures sitting on the hood before it's gone? I fell in love with it the moment I heard about it on the ad, and I really want to check it out before it's gone. I know it has to be very appealing in person."

"Umm. Yeah. Sure. When were you thinking about coming in? She's supposed to be in before closing."

"What time do you close today?"

"I close up at five o'clock this evening."

"How about around four or four-fiteen?"

"That should work."

"Okay, Bye Jay. I'll see you soon," Tash said in a seductive tone.

"Okay. See you then."

4:13 P.M.

"Hello, welcome to Jay's Classic Sports Ride, I'm Jay. How can I help you ma'am?"

"Damn you fine," the woman said, sizing me up. I couldn't help but to share my pearly whites with her in return for her compliment. Before I had a chance to respond, the woman continued...

"Hi Jay, it's so nice to meet you. My name is Tash. I spoke with you earlier on the phone about coming in to look at the six second, manual transmission, peanut butter sports car with Melanin Muscle. Is now a good time?" Tash asked flirtatiously.

Tash entered the shop alone and looked sexier than a muthafucka. But, something about her told me she came in looking to buy this Peanut Butter V8 Supercharged Dick with the Hemi, with just her looks. She was one of those women who dressed very nicely and carried a designer bag with not a dollar in it. She reminded me of a, "I got you on the first or the fifteenth" kind of woman. But, she was someone you couldn't resist because she was just that damn cold. Tash walked with hella confidence and no one could tell her anything.

Tash's hair was pulled back into a tight eighteen-inch ponytail. She wore a mini white high-waisted button-front pencil skirt, with a soft blush pink top, a pair of light pink vinyl ankle-strap heel sandals, with a pink and white Balenciaga top-handle satchel bag.

She was smoking hot! Her legs were dipped in Johnson's baby oil, her body was snatched, and she was in my shop by her lonesome. Why would a woman looking that fine come here just to look at a ride she isn't able to purchase? And with no chaperone? I knew something could not be right. But hey, who am I to judge? A woman wants what she wants, right?

Stumbling over my words, because of how gorgeous she presented herself, "Yes, Ta-Tash, I...I remember you. Pleasure to meet you. Thanks for coming in."

I extended my hand for a handshake and she gently placed her smooth right hand inside of mine. She bit her bottom lip and gave my hand a gentle shake.

"It's so nice to meet you. I'm happy you allowed me to come in to check out the car today, even though someone has already beat me to the prize," Tash exclaimed.

"My pleasure. It was the least I could do, seeing how excited you were about the car and hoping to make it your own."

"What a nice display room you have here, Jay."

"Two Can Play that Game"   *Jameel Davis*

"Thanks, Tash. You look amazing by the way," I managed to squeeze out. "Would you like to browse the showroom before we head back?"

"Oh, thank you, Daddy. I mean…Jay," Tash blushed. "No thank you, I know you will be closing up soon and I want to spend as much time as I can with your dick, I mean looking at — and taking pictures with — your rare fully-loaded ride before the soon-to-be owner comes in and drives it away for good," Tash said sarcastically.

"Alright, I understand. Let's get you to it. Right this way," I indicated.

I slightly turned backward toward the left and held out my left hand signaling for Tash to walk ahead of me. She model-walked past me and led the way to the back display room. I paused momentarily, taking in the luscious view of her bouncy ass that was swaying from side to side with each strut in those pink heel sandals. I just knew she didn't have anything beneath that white mini skirt by the way her ass dribbled freely. My dick immediately swelled up trying to burst out of my gray slacks, like a caged animal. He wanted to attack the basket, turn that ass over, and let her rain her bodily fluids all over him.

"Two Can Play that Game"

Jameel Davis

"Are you the only one in today, Jay?" Tash asked curiously.

"Yes, just me today," I responded.

Tash sensed I wasn't following right behind her. She stopped and turned around with one of her hands resting on her hip. I quickly turned my head as if I was looking outside the door. "Jay are you coming? Yes, I'm coming. I thought I saw something outside," I lied. I started walking in her direction and Tash turned around and kept on walking.

I decided to free-ball today, and the head of my dick just kept banging on the zipper of my pants, trying to get beneath that white mini skirt and plunge her wet walls. When we reached the back display room, I turned away from Tash, unzipped my pants and my V8 lunged full throttle, right out of the garage. It was charged up, spit-shined, and ready to roar. I turned back to face Tash, "is this the ride you heard about and that brought you in today?" I asked, as I watched her eyes drop from my eyes to my golden brown hood and shiny front bumper with amazement.

"Two Can Play that Game"   _Jameel Davis_

"Yes, that-is-exactly-what-I-came-here-to-see," Tash said slowly in a sexy, seductive tone. Your dick looks so fucking good. I would love to lick the brown right off of it. I was sold after hearing the ad, and being here now to see it in person, just made my pussy very wet. That golden brown V8 exceeded my pussy's imagination and she's throbbing with excitement. Jay, nothing is in her way and any second now, there will be a puddle forming right where I am standing. Can I sit on the hood and you take me for a quick spin?"

"I'm not sure about that, the owner should be here soon and I'm sure she would want it in the same condition she purchased it in. And besides, I don't think you can handle HorsePower. You don't seem like the sportscar type," I laughed.

"What? What kind of car do you think is my type?

"A Honda CRV," I laughed.

"Haha, very funny Jay. Don't let this skirt and these heels fool you. I can handle that ride," she pointed at my dick with her head.

"I don't know, Tash!"

"Are you the only one in today, Jay?" Tash asked curiously.

"Yes, just me today," I responded.

Tash sensed I wasn't following right behind her. She stopped and turned around with one of her hands resting on her hip. I quickly turned my head as if I was looking outside the door. "Jay are you coming? Yes, I'm coming. I thought I saw something outside," I lied. I started walking in her direction and Tash turned around and kept on walking.

I decided to free-ball today, and the head of my dick just kept banging on the zipper of my pants, trying to get beneath that white mini skirt and plunge her wet walls. When we reached the back display room, I turned away from Tash, unzipped my pants and my V8 lunged full throttle, right out of the garage. It was charged up, spit-shined, and ready to roar. I turned back to face Tash, "is this the ride you heard about and that brought you in today?" I asked, as I watched her eyes drop from my eyes to my golden brown hood and shiny front bumper with amazement.

"Two Can Play that Game"

Jameel Davis

"Come on, Jay, please can I? It will be quick. You said I can take pictures on it. I want to take pictures sitting on the hood and in the driver's seat. You know a lady has to make her moment memorable with a one-of-a-kind ride, you know?"

"Look Jay, there's no better way to create this memory than to sit my soft ass all on it, get behind the wheel, and let you take me for a quick spin. Look at me; I know you want me to sit this pussy on it and ride it like a rodeo. I'll even give you the honor of taking the pictures for me and you can keep the ones you love most."

"Ummm."

"Jay, before you answer, technically it's not hers just yet. It's still here…and she's not. She put down a deposit to hold it. Look at me, I can pay for it in full right now," Tash said, tracing her hands over her breasts, down her hips and waist, across her ass, back around to the front of her thighs and up her skirt.

"If she really wanted it that bad, she would have been here sooner than later. I'm just saying. Look Jay, I just want to sit on it, take my pictures, and let you drive me around the block real quick. She can have it."

"Two Can Play that Game"   *Jameel Davis*

"So can I sit on it, take my pictures, and we take it for a spin or what?"

"I guess you are right. It's not hers until she pays for it fully. Look, you can sit on this dick and I'll take you for a quick spin, so you can hold onto these memories for the rest of your life. But, it has to be quick and you have to be careful not to scratch up the paint job or smear the paint."

"I'm already wet and ready."

"And Jay, you don't have to worry about me messing up your pretty ass dick, damn. I brought a pair of golden gloves to put over it. I will handle it quickly and with care. Trust me!"

"It is a six-second car, right?' Tash confirmed.

"Yes it is," I replied.

So let's take it from zero to sixty. Let me pull it around back and drive, so you can hit all the right spots and capture all the right angles before she gets here. You will enjoy me riding you around.``

"Jay, when I pull it around back, I'm going to turn around so you can hop on in. As soon as you get inside me, I'll push the pedal to the medal and burn some rubber — cuming quickly all over your big, sexy-ass dick. After hitting a few corners, just hop out in mid-stroke and snap a few pictures with this ass you've been drooling over, twerked up on the hood. Use your free hand to grip my ass tight. And If you are really up to it, put the camera in slow-motion, slide your dick back inside me, and slam it on home. I'll cum — back to back, reset your odometer, and my test drive will be over before she notices anything out of place."

"Alright, I'm convinced. Come get the keys and put your seatbelt on; I don't want you flying out the windshield if you collide with something or have to slam on the brakes," I chuckled.

Tash had a mouthpiece and I liked that shit. She wasn't leaving without taking this supercharged hemi dick on a mini road trip. She may have heard it on the radio, or seen it on the video, but she ain't never experienced anything like what I was about to show her.

Welcome to the Daytona 500, Tash. Let the fun begin, I said to myself.

"Two Can Play that Game"

Jameel Davis

Tash pulled out her phone and a Trojan Bareskin Magnum from her pink and white Balenciaga bag and walked over to where I stood. She turned her cell phone camera on to portrait mode and placed it in my hand. Tash quickly ripped the golden Trojan Magnum wrapper off with her teeth and removed the rolled up condom from the package with one hand. My dick smiled instantly at the sight of it; it was something I had never seen a woman do before.
Tash moved closer to me and rolled the glove over my bumper, down to the base of my dick with one hand. That was some sexy shit, and it felt so good letting her massage it onto my dick.

Once Tash had the glove snuggled all the way on my dick, she lifted her skirt over her ass. Tash then took hold of my dick and held onto it with her left hand and pulled me around the back of her, as she turned her ass around to meet my supersized machine. One at a time, Tash placed her knees up on the black leather seat cushions that sat in front of the window. She bent over forward and buried her face into the back pillow of the chair and held the arm of the chair with her free hand. Tash slowly inserted my head deep inside of her wet pussy. Once I reached the bottom of her, Tash lifted her head, placed both hands on the chair pillow for support, and tried to take off on it like she indicated earlier — nearly hurting herself.

Tash screamed, "ouch," and jumped off my dick and hit her forehead on the window.

"Take it easy, this ain't that Honda CRV. I told you, you couldn't handle it and I told you to put your seatbelt on didn't I?" I said, laughing.

"Shut up! I can handle it. It's been a while," Tash yelled.

I could tell Tash hasn't had her oil checked in a minute either. She knew she couldn't handle it right off the bat, but insisted on fighting through the pressure.

I didn't have all day to be training some pussy that obviously needed some training wheels and driver's ed — and whose owner was talking mad shit about how she can handle any ride. So I took over the test drive.

I grabbed her ass with one hand and pulled her back down towards me, resting her head back on the chair pillow. She held the arms of the chair as I placed my hand on the lower end of her back, pressing down on it — making her arch her back and toot her ass up. I spread her thick left ass cheek with my left hand, took hold of my fully erect dick with my right hand, and slowly worked a third of my dick back inside of her pussy. Once I was back inside, I palmed both of her ass cheeks and slowly stroked her pussy until she was able to handle and enjoy it.

"Two Can Play that Game"   _Jameel Davis_

I switched the camera to slow motion mode and stroked her pink lining delicately. The horsepower kicked in and I pounded her pavement with my melainated hemi, as she contracted and expanded her pussy muscles faster and faster on my dick, cuming loudly on it again.

I was having a ball serving her this roaring dick.

I wanted to see if Tash was ready to take it for a spin. So, I slid out and moved over so we could switch seats. Tash stood up and I sat down on the damped leather cushions she had soaked up. Once I was in the passenger seat, Tash climbed onto the driver seat, hit the clutch, and kicked my thick golden gear stick that was firm and ready for her enjoyment, right into fourth gear. Tash took the wheel and pushed the pedal to the medal, trying to peel the rubber off this dick. Tash dribbled her ass up and down on me, twirling her hips out of control. She clenched her hands on my shoulder, clenched her thighs against mine, and squeezed her moist pussy tightly around my dick. Tash rode me hard and fast, raining her warm droplets all over my hood.

I wailed and moaned in pleasure, tensing my body up preparing to fill the inside of the Trojan condom she had rolled on me, with a load of cream. Before I reached the point of no return, Tash hopped up off my dick, kneeled down, and quickly snatched the condom off.

"Two Can Play that Game"

Jameel Davis

Her breaths increased heavily and after a few deep slow strokes, I felt her pussy tighten quickly around my dick and her body tense up, secreting more of her juices on me. She gasped and moaned deeply, holding her breath. Suddenly, her pussy muscles rapidly expanded and contracted on my dick as she came loudly all over the Magnum — relaxing the muscles in her body. Tash cried the sexiest moan ever, as if she hummed the melody of a beautiful song.

She was right about cuming quickly as soon as I was inside of her.

Tash releasing that powerful orgasm she had locked away like that turned me all-the-way-on. I gradually pressed my foot further down on the accelerator, increasing my speed inside her walls. Before I knew it, I was ramping my shiny bumper into her walls at 60 MPH, burning the rubber off this Supercharged V8 Hemi. Her loud moans became muffled as she sung into the pillow, then grew louder as she lifted her head and her sweet melodies vibrated off the window — fogging it up with her Doublemint breath.

I paused inside of her pussy mid-stroke, grabbed her phone, and snapped several pictures of the head of my dick resting inside of her cozy pussy lips. e.

Tash drove her face in my lap and wrapped her lips around my dick. She used her right hand to pull the skin down on my dick and waxed my dick with her thick saliva. She quickly bobbed her head up and down, driving the head of my dick deeper and deeper into the back of her throat. My eyes rolled in the back of my head before shutting tightly, my muscles tensed up — and I gasped and held in my cum as long as I could.

When I felt I could not hold my cum back much longer, I turned my head towards the doorway and opened my eyes — aahing loud as fuck, as I shot a thick creamy load into Tash's mouth. I sat motionless, watching the woman standing in the doorway stare down at us, as Tash continued to squeeze her powerful jaws tighter and tighter around my dick, increasing the speed of her neck until she slurped up and swallowed the last drop of me.

My Way by Giorgio Armani

Curious & Adventurous

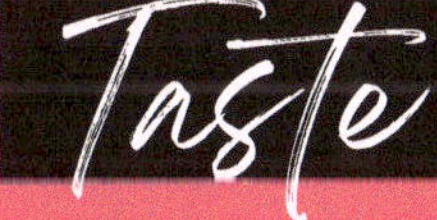

Nude Silk Robe, Blue Laced Thongs, Johnson's Baby Oil, The Rose, Dimmed Lights, Plushed Rug, Kitchen Island/Floor,

Alcohol infused whipped cream, chocolate covered grapes, ice cubes, fruit infused wine

Girls Want Girls by Drake

Scan & Listen

<u>LES-BE-HONEST</u>

Girls like Girls and Girls love Girls.

But Girls are afraid to love on Girls
the way they wish Girls could love
on them.

Girl get your Girl, you can't go wrong.
Twirling Tongues and laced thongs paired
with the perfect song, "Let's Get it On."

She likes dick, and even loves it too.
Well, so do you.

Get you some too — with her.

Or don't get any at all.

Slide in her DM, shoot her a text,
Girl, make your move.

She's on your mind and she thinks
you're fine, she's been waiting on you.

"Two Can Play that Game"

Jameel Davis

Oh, she has a man! Well, save him
a piece of cake too.

Or just watch him devour hers
and join in too.

She's on your mind and she thinks
you're fine, she's been waiting on you.

Oh, she has a man! Well, save him
a piece of cake too.

Or just watch him devour hers
and join in too.

Set your pussy free, she's waiting for you
on the other end of the speed dial.

Pick up the phone, she's already bored.

Don't forget your camera and press
record.

Be a Star in your own Lesbian Porn.

"Two Can Play that Game"   _Jameel Davis_

Chapter 5

"Lick it Up Daddy"

"LICK IT UP DADDY"

WATERFALL

"I'm looking forward to bending you over on your stomach, palming your cheeks,

and holding my tongue up underneath your melting clit, watching your love drip slowly all on it. I can't wait to lick my lips after swallowing your love and driving my flickering tongue back and forth and all around on those peachy lips, sucking the sweet juices from between them."

"Lick it Up Daddy"

Jameel Davis

Sex-Esteem
DADDY
" NOT ALL DICK GET CROWNED "DADDY."

DADDY'S GIRL

There's nothing like a woman's love for daddy—'s—dick.

The way she hugs daddy-dick, kisses daddy-dick, and sits on daddy's dick like it's Christmas time, is one of the greatest feelings in the world. I love it when she treats daddy-dick as if I'm the one who gave her life, bought her every gift she has ever asked for, and raised her to be the amazing woman she has grown to become.

No disrespect to her father, but I love my baby girl too. And — her pussy tastes so—fucking—good, feels so—fucking—good, and she sucks daddy's—dick, so—fucking—good.

I'm grateful for her father and give him the highest praise for our baby girl. But, she sounds so much better calling me daddy when I am deep down inside of her pussy making her cum uncontrollably while moaning, "I love you daddy," than when she calls him Daddy and tells him she loves him.

"Lick it Up Daddy"

Jameel Davis

Aroma

(Male) Acqua Di Gio (Female) Flora by Gucci

Mood

Sunday Funday

Sight

(Male) Blue Nike Basketball Shorts, White T-shirt, White Nike Socks, Black Nike Flip Flops, (Female) Jet Black Silk Press, Red Bodycon Dress, Black Pumps,

Taste

Bottomless Mimosas, Fresh Pineapples, Watermelon, Laffy Taffy

Sound

Flawless (Remix) by Beyoncé (Feat. Nicki Minaj)

Scan & Listen

LOLLIPOPPIN

It's Sunday afternoon and Lele just crept in the house from her hair appointment —headed right for the kitchen.

When she entered the kitchen, she found me standing at the sink wearing a pair of blue Nike basketball shorts, a white A-shirt, a pair of white Nike crew socks and a pair of black Nike flip flops — cleaning our dinner dishes from the night before.

"Hey handsome, I'm home. Did you miss me?" she said in her flirtatious voice.

I was startled at the sound of her sexy tone.

Before I could turn around to meet the beautiful woman who placed her wet lips around my warm dick as I was sleeping that morning — and who kissed me goodbye on her way out of the door — the sound of her soft voice, the smell of her sweet perfume, and the quick thought of how good she sucked my dick that morning, instantly got my dick hard — again.

I quickly turned my head away from the plate I was holding in front of me to meet her seductive eyes;

"Hey Le-Baby, how was your salon appointment?" I asked, smiling.

"It wasn't as amazing as the service I gave myself for breakfast this morning, but it was good," she chuckled. "Do you like my hair?" she asked anxiously.

"I think the jet-black looks great on you. I really like it. Did you leave her a tip, because she hooked my baby up?"

"Aww thank you, daddy. And no, she cut too much of my hair off when she was clipping my ends and I told her not to," she replied, rolling her neck.

"I can't tell any of it is missing; your hair looks full to me Le-Baby, and you look fine than a muthafucka. You know if you drink sixty-four ounces of water every day and eat your pineapples, your hair will be back where you want it," I encouraged her with a big Kool-Aid smile.

"And you know what those pineapples do to that pussy, don't you?" I added, laughing.

"Pussy super sweet, you be tasting like pineapples."

"Ok D'Von, If you like it, then I love it — silly," Lele giggled.

"By the way, my mouth is dry and I'm thirsty," she said, while biting her bottom lip, clenching her legs together, and studying deeply at my dick print that was poking out the center of my basketball shorts.

My dick started bulging at the sight of her body's reactions, causing my shorts to rise and fall. Lele knew just what to say to get him knocking, attempting to break free from the blue nylon fabric.

"I see someone is wide awake and excited to see me," she said, nodding her head, pointing at my nudging dick. You must have known I came back specially for that thick, long, caramelized dick — huh D'Von?

"Hell yeah! You know it. We both are happy to see you; we missed you," I replied, sizing her fine ass up in that red bodycon dress she wore that hugged every curve on her body. Complementing her dress, Lele wore a pair of black pumps she had kicked off to the side, and her hair was shoulder-length, and silk pressed. She was eye-candy and I was ready to unwrap that watermelon Laffy Taffy.

"Come give us a hug and drink from our coconut fountain again," I said, sliding my hands inside of my shorts, massaging my hands all over my hard dick.

Lele slowly walked on over to where I stood. I opened my arms, welcoming her inside of them. Lele placed her arms around my neck as I placed my arms around her, pressing her body tightly onto mine. I tilted my head down, locking my pink lips onto her full lips. I traced my hands down her backside until I rolled them onto her delicate ass cheeks — that had revealed themselves after she stretched her arms up to hug me. I palmed both of her golden brown glazed buns and lifted them — bringing her onto her tippy-toes. I eased two of my clean fingers between her slippery lips as we kissed passionately for several seconds. Le slipped her thick peppermint flavored tongue inside of my mouth as I continued playing with her clitoris — squirting her watery juices all down my fingers.

Our tongues intertwined and we sucked on each other's lips and tongue until the peppermint flavor was gone. I rubbed her clitoris and stroked her G-spot until a puddle of her treasures formed at our feet.

Lele moaned loudly as my dick nudged repeatedly on her stomach, desperate to get inside of her. She felt my dick's anticipation and pulled away from me to show him some attention.

"Lick it Up Daddy"

Jameel Davis

Lele placed her hand inside of my shorts and placed her warm hand around my hard dick, slowly pulling it out. Lele squatted down on the kitchen rug and slid my boxers and shorts down to my ankles. I stepped out of my boxers and shorts as my dick hovered over her head like halo. Lele held on to my fully erect dick and bowed her head to bless it — my balls and its warm creamy contents — like she usually does, before guiding me deep into her wet mouth.

"Bless me, oh Lord and this beautiful dick, attached to this beautiful Black man, and it's warm, sweet, cum, which I am about to receive from his body. Please bless these amazing balls and help my mouth to use his load to nourish my body and keep my skin healthy. In the Holy Goddess of Pussy name I pray, Awomen."

Lele lifted her head and the head of my dick was within centimeters of her lips. I reached down and pulled her hair off her face, taking a fist full of it and holding it on top of her head. She opened her mouth and quickly guided my dick across her tongue into the back of her mouth, closing her soft lips down on it. My knees went limp and I gasped in pleasure. Her mouth felt just as good — if not better — than that morning.

"Lick it Up Daddy"

Jameel Davis

Lele quickly moved my dick in and out of her wet mouth. I could tell she was thirsty.

"Damn Le-Baby, slow down. Daddy-Dick is feeling too good and I'm not ready to cum yet," I moaned.

Lele paused momentarily, *"I love sucking Daddy-Dick. It's so good to me. I want you to cum all in my mouth and all on my face,"* she said softly while looking up into my eyes.

Lele's words got me more excited — my dick throbbed and grew larger. She placed my dick back inside of her mouth and continued serving me some bomb-ass head, slurping and slobbering away as she massaged my balls. I looked down in between her thighs and I saw her pussy running like a dripping faucet onto the rug.

"Lollipoppin', No Panties in the way."

Lele brought me up on my tippy-toes sucking the brakes off of my dick. My toes started cracking from tensing up. I was moments away from filling her mouth back up with more of my warm creamy frosting.

"Lick it Up Daddy"   *Jameel Davis*

"Le, Suck it Faster!
Go Faster.
Faster.
Faster."

Each time I said, *"faster,"* Lele's head moved faster and her jaws squeezed tighter — sucking me out of control. She went crazy on the dick and I hadn't had my dick sucked like that in what felt like ages. I was deeply in love with how she was pleasing me with *"No Hands."* Her mouth felt like heaven on my dick and I could barely keep my eyes open.

Lele felt my warm cum getting ready to protrude out of my long, super horny dick. She took her mouth off of my dick and moved back slightly to catch the nut.

"Cum all in my mouth and all over my face daddy," she said seductively. *"I know daddy tastes good and I can't wait to feel your warm love all on my face."*

"Serve it to me in my mouth, D'Von."

Lele opened her mouth wide open, tilted her head back, and stuck out her tongue. She grasped the back of my knees tightly with her hands and watched as I squeezed and stroked my dick with her saliva, faster, and harder — aiming to unleash the powerful beast I had been desperately waiting to release deep into her mouth.

"I'm bout-to-cum, I'm bout-to-cum,' I cried in satisfaction.

I closed my eyes, held my breath, contracted my pelvic floor muscles, and shot a load of my warm love all in her mouth and all over her face.

"Ahhhhh, fuckkkk.
Shitttt. That felt so good.
Thank you baby,"
I said breathing heavily.

I opened my eyes and noticed I had gotten some in her hair and eye. *"Sorry about your hair and your eye Le,"* I said, laughing."

Lele made sure she sucked that last drop out of me before responding.

"Anything for my Big Daddy," Lele smiled. And, It's ok D'Von, that's what I wanted you to do," she grinned. Lele licked my cum off of her lips and smiled once more,

"Mmm. Daddy Tastes So Good."

"*Lick it Up Daddy*"   *Jameel Davis*

Lele slowly stood back up on her feet and attempted to pull her dress back down. There was no way I was going to let her faucet just leak without me sucking her well dry. I took hold of Lele's hands and placed them back around my neck. I lifted her bodycon dress up over her bouncy ass and placed my hands back on it. I grabbed her cheeks and lifted her up on the edge of the marble island. Lele opened her legs and her pussy continued to drip onto the smooth surface — forming puddles between her thick slippery thighs. Lele pulled me closer to her and reached her right hand down and grabbed my dick that was still hungry for more of her. She widened her legs and I stood up on my toes so she could rub the head of my dick back and forth against the opening of her melting lips.

As Lele began slapping my dick faster and faster against her clitoris, splashing her crystal juices on both of us, I tilted her chin up with my index finger to join her lips with mine again. I slid my hand down to her waist, leaned my head down, and began kissing her passionately on the lips. I moved my right hand around to her lower back and supported her as I traced my lips and tongue along her neckline, while caressing her B-cup breasts with my left hand.

"Lick it Up Daddy"   _Jameel Davis_

Lele suddenly placed her left hand on the back of my head, guiding my mouth to stimulate the hot spot on the left side of her neck. She rotated my head in a circular motion as I pressed my lips and tongue harder onto her spot. Lele slapped and rubbed my dick harder and harder against her clitoris as she moaned and twirled her hips on the marble surface.

Lele turned her face toward mine, pulled my mouth from her neck and plunged her juicy tongue deep into my mouth. I twirled my tongue onto hers and suckled softly on her bottom lip, making her more aroused. Her breathing intensified and her body started quivering. She was working up a powerful orgasm to release on me and this marble island top.

She scooted closer to the edge of the island and rested her heels up on the island top. My dick continued to rattle her clitoris as our lips and tongue intertwined. Lele grinded her booty faster on the surface. I took my dick from her hand, stood up higher on my tippy-toes and slipped my dick right inside of her throbbing wet walls. Lele gripped my waist with both of her hands and threw her pelvis into fourth gear as I plunged my dick deeper and deeper into her squirting walls.

Before Lele could cum on my thrusting dick, I slid my dick out of her snuggly moist pussy, laid her back on the island, and buried my face deep between her thighs — sucking the juices off of her peachy lips.

"Oooh D'Von."
"Oooh D'Von."
"D'Von."
"Right there Daddy,"

Lele, moaned loudly.

Lele took slow, long, and deep breaths. She placed both of her hands on the back of my head and closed her thighs tightly on my ears. I couldn't hear anything but the sound of me licking the flavor off of her clitoris. She threw her hips back into fourth gear — feeding me her warm, tasty, pineapple-flavored pussy.

"Oooh D'Von."
"Oooh D'Von."
"My pussy feels so fucking good."

"Mmm. Pussy so sweet," my words vibrated off of her lips.

"Yes, this pussy is sweet for you, Daddy," she whispered.

I broke Lele's wedge with my hands, freeing my neck. She opened her thighs and held them open for me to enter. I quickly climbed up on the island top and inserted my dick back inside of her. I pressed my dick against her clitoris, overstimulating it, as I moved deep and fast — in and out of her squeaky wet pussy.

"Lick it Up Daddy"

Jameel Davis

"*I'm cumming daddy, I'm cumming daddy,*" Lele screamed in elation.

Lele's body tensed up and she inhaled deeply. She contracted her spongy walls around my swollen dick and exhaled, rinsing me with ounces of her warm love. Her body relaxed and her love slowly flowed down to my ball-sack,dripping off onto the island.

I laid on top of Lele and rested my lips onto hers. While taking in our moment of affection, her pussy continued to throb as I rested my hard dick inside of her.

#POUNDCAKE

I never know what's happening between the thighs of my woman when I'm not head first in them, until I lick and stroke deeply inside of her thighs, soaking up her panties, the sheets, car seats, countertops, couches, my face, stomach, and fully erect dick. And right now, I can't wait to squirm head first like a python between her thighs, licking the melting icing from her "Pineapple Upside Down Pound-Cake" — placing my tongue back inside both sets of her lips for us to enjoy together.

So Delicious Girl!

Text me #Cake Ready Bae, hit send and I'm arriving to help you arrive with my soft, pink lips circulating all around your clitoris, while my tongue is submerged deeply inside of you.

Text me #Cake Ready Bae and hit send, so I can turn that cake upside down how you like it and #-It, as your pineapple frosting drizzles nicely down the shaft of this dick — enjoying our dessert together.

"Lick it Up Daddy"

Jameel Davis

SHE ONLY WANTS ME BECAUSE I EAT HER PUSSY DELICIOUSLY!

And that's okay because I absolutely love when my pink lips and warm-twisted-stuttering-tongue slurp and spit all on her when I talk my shit — all in her face.

Use me all you want!

(Female) Butter, Honey, Vanilla and Lavender (Male) Midnight by Bath & Body Works

Sweet Tooth

(Male) Navy Blue Basketball Shorts, Gray Gildan Boxer Briefs, Black Puma Slides, Navy Blue Puma Hoodie, (Female) Short Ivory Robe with Flowy Sleeves, Hair in Loose Bun, Moonlight, Lake, Patio Deck, Red Sports Car

Blue Moon, Andy Chocolate Mint Candies, Honey LemonHalls, Spearmint Gum,

Superstar by Usher, Rock Me Baby by BB King

Scan & Listen

Scan & Listen

MIDNIGHT

I'll never forget the time I sat Shay fine ass up on the hood of my 2020 Candy Red Chevy Camaro, and ate her pussy under the stars and crescent moonlight.

"Lick it Up Daddy"   Jameel Davis

Let me tell you how all of this freaky shit went down...

 It was a Friday night and the clock had just struck midnight. I was up laying in my bed with my hand resting inside of my navy blue basketball shorts — watching Violet's fine ass in Nappily Ever After. My mouth began to water for something soft-smooth-warm-juicy and sweet, and I needed a midnight snack before I called it a night.

 So, I hit up Exotic Treats. Shay's number is saved under that name in my phone.

 Shay always keeps her bakery fresh, with her pastry ready to be devoured. She cannot slide her Laced Vicky Panties down off of her fine ass without her pussy's sweet aroma intoxicating my nostrils first. Her pussy has its own distinct lavender smell and it be tasting so fucking-good. It's almost as if she maranates her pussy in butter, honey, vanilla, and lavender extract. Shay keeps Ms. Squeaky looking-feeling-smelling and tasting so amazing. Her whole entire being is so delicious. Everytime I finish my treat, she gives me a pair of her Secret Panties to hang over my rearview mirror to use as a car freshener. If she's wearing them.

 Shay is very sweet and special to me, and I had to do something extra exotic to her pussy that night.

 I grabbed my phone, brought it towards my face, and used my Kool-Aid smile to unlock it. I slid my hand inside of my new pair of gray Gildan boxer-briefs I got for Father's Day, and rested it on my warm-soft dick. Before I could open my contacts to dial Shay, a DM notification popped up from her. My dick jerked quickly with excitement.

 I clicked on my Instagram DM notification, and my eyes met her freshly waxed Puma. I knew she just got it done earlier that day. It wasn't the kind of boomerang she would normally post on IG to attract new clients to her best friend (who is an esthetician), it was a visual indicating she wanted my face buried deep between her peanut butter chocolate thighs.

 I could tell by the way her legs were wedged open as she compressed her brown cheeks on the thunder white granite vanity sink in the bathroom. I damn near licked the screen on my phone, her pussy looked so pulchritudinous (pul·chri·tu·di·nous).

 Shay's LED "Bakery Open" sign was accompanied by an emoji cupcake and the word, "Sweet Tooth" followed by a question mark.

"Lick it Up Daddy"

Jameel Davis

"Fresh out the oven, jelly-filled with icing," I replied to Shay with a drooling mouth and chocolate covered doughnut with sprinkles emoji.

The licking lips emoji accompanied Shay's response, "Baked to perfection with slimy-vanilla-filling made with extra love for you tonight. Now, come on and get it before it cools off," Shay demanded.

"I'm grabbing my oven mitts now," I replied with emoji gloves and a smirk emoji.

And leave it unwrapped.

"Kk."

I received an iMessage from Shay seconds after. She had shared her current location with me. She knew once I got off of the 305 exit, I would be calling her for directions like I normally would do.

I jumped up out of bed, slid my feet into my black Puma slides, snatched my navy blue Puma hoodie that was hanging on my closet door, threw it on, and ran down the steps. I entered the kitchen, grabbed a couple pieces of Andy Chocolate Mint Candies, honey lemon flavored Halls, and a sandwich bag filled with ice cubes.

I grabbed my 2020 Chevy Camaro Smart Keyless Entry w/Engine Start remote off the Kitchen counter and hurried out the side door.

I walked around, opened my driver door and sat inside of my candy red 2-door coupe. I buckled my seatbelt, activated the push to start, let the sunroof back, threw it in reverse, and peeled out of my driveway.

As I cruised south down the boulevard, I turned up Under by Pleasure P (who was whispering through my door speakers) and popped two pieces of mint candy into my mouth. I had to freshen my breath before my arrival because I loved whenever Shay and I met up, and she inserted her Spearmint-flavor tongue inside of my mouth and sucked the chocolate and mint flavor off of mine.

My tastebuds continued to water as I reminisced about how watery her mouth was when we last kissed — and when she slid my dick slowly in and out of her soft, bubbly, two-tone, pink and brown lips with ice and honey lemon-flavored Halls.
Shay sucked my dick sexy and with passion. I came within minutes, nutting one of the slowest, longest, and greatest nuts I had ever released — down her throat. I can still see her face, hair pulled tight into a ponytail, licking her shiny lips and moaning, "mmm it tastes so good, Daddy."

"_Lick it Up Daddy_"   _Jameel Davis_

I drove for about twenty minutes bumping panty-wetters through my car stereo system by artists R. Kelly, Trey Songz, Ginuwine, Tyrese, and Chris Brown. I exited the 305 off Route 2 in Eastlake, Ohio. Shay lives in a beautiful house right on Lake Erie, which happens to be right in her backyard. She has a mini dock leading out to the water, and a pair of jet-skis. I've been over to Shay's house a few times to pick her up and to drop her off, but never really stayed long enough to hangout. We always ended up at other exotic places for our tasty encounters.

I decided to make her own backyard our wet spot that night.

I arrived at Shay's house and pulled into her driveway. As I drove to the back of her house, Tyrese - Turn Ya Out rattled her windows. I put the car in park and looked up through my sunroof to her balcony door that led to her master bedroom. I saw her silhouette approaching the glass patio door. Shay reached the door and I watched as she peeked through the curtain before opening it. Shay came out onto the patio wearing a short ivory robe with flowy sleeves. Her hair was pulled off of her face into a loose bun. She approached the banister, looked down, and met my eyes looking up to her.

"Hello gorgeous," I smiled.

Shay flapped her fingers and smiled back at me.

"Ooo hi Jamal, you look good as fuck in that 'Maro.' My pussy just tingled looking at you through the roof from here," she said, squeezing her thighs together and biting her fingernail.

"Can you take me for a spin after I put some of this brown sugar on your tooth?" Shay asked with excitement.

"Thank you baby. I'm glad you like it," I replied.

"I see you holding it back; don't let that cream filling seep out just yet. I want to nibble on it and let the melted icing glide down my mouth first,' I said, sucking my bottom lip.

Shay blushed.

"I'll take you on a night cruise, as-soon-as I am finished with my midnight snack," I said, licking my lips.

"You look as elegant as a Vendela Ivory Rose from down here; I can't wait to hold open your legs and place my thirsty mouth all on you tonight."

"Ooo, I can't wait either," Shay said, squeezing her thighs tighter.

"That is my shit. You don't know nothing about Turn Ya Out Jamal," she shouted.

"You know Tyrese is the homie. He's always helping me get my tongue ready to dance on that sweet, throbbing pussy of yours. Now, come on before it gets cold. Remember?" I said, licking my lips with a smirk.

"I'll be down in a minute silly, and I hope you are ready, because she's unwrapped and ready to wipe your face clean," Shay said, laughing as she walked back inside.

I switched the vibe from R&B to blues as I waited for Shay to come outside. R&B sets the tone and can lead you to an amazing night, but eating some good pussy and fucking to the blues just hit differently — especially when outside is your playground and the woman you are pleasuring is both elegant and tasty.

I turned the volume down on my stereo, turned off my LED fog lights, opened my driver door, and stepped out of the car. I closed the car door behind me and walked to the front of the car which was facing the direction of the lake. I stood leaning on the hood of the car and waited for Shay to come out of the house.

"Lick it Up Daddy"

Jameel Davis

Shay exited the back door of her house shortly after and my dick grew bigger and bigger, trying to protrude itself out of my basketball shorts as she headed towards my direction. I could not wait to untie that ivory robe she wore that had my warm dessert wrapped beneath it.

I stood up off the car and met Shay at my passenger side; she approached me wearing a bright Kool-Aid smile. When she got close enough, she threw her arms around my neck, and squeezed me tightly. I placed my arms around her waist and rested both of my hands on the cuffs of her cheeks where the robe had ended — and squeezed her booty softly.

"Nice Oven Mitts Daddy," she laughed.

Shay lifted her chin off of my shoulder and positioned her lips within centimeters of mine. She placed her lips gently onto mine as I kissed her passionately in return. As I knew she would do, she placed her Spearmint flavor tongue inside of my mouth and sucked the Andy Chocolate Mint flavor slowly off of my tongue. We kissed for a good minute, exchanging mint saliva before separating our lips.

"*Lick it Up Daddy*"

Jameel Davis

Shay hugged me once more, resting her chin back on my shoulder. She then drove her nose across my neck, sniffing the Midnight Collection from Bath & Body Works.

"You smell good, Mal." What are you wearing? She asked curiously.

"Midnight from Bath and Body," I replied.

"Midnight at midnight? How ironic," she giggled.

"Right, I didn't realize I showered with it and lathered the body cream on me until after you asked."

Shay looked over my shoulder and acknowledged the Camaro once more, "nice—taste."

And I replied, "not as tasty as you," sliding her robe between her cheeks as I gripped her booty more firmly this time.

The air was warm, the water was calm, and not another soul was in sight. It was just the two of us, the clear navy sky, the crescent moonlight, and the sounds of BB King - Rock Me Baby playing softly through my car stereo.

"Lick it Up Daddy"

Jameel Davis

Shay eased her perky, aroused breasts off of my chest, separating our bodies, and reached her hand out for my hand. I relaxed my hand inside of her oily palm as she turned and walked away, pulling me along with her. As we headed in the direction of her house, I surveyed her backside, her thick shiny thighs, and the way her Reese's Peanut Butter Cups swayed back and forth, peeking at me from beneath her ivory robe. I thought about stopping her in mid-walk, bending her over, and making her touch her toes so I could kneel down and submerge my forehead between her milk chocolate buns, French kissing her cocoa butter lips, sucking the slimy-vanilla-filling from deep inside of her.

The thought of me bending her over right in her driveway to satisfy my sweet-tooth made my dick harder. I wanted to bend her over but not with her hovering over her knees in the driveway. I wanted to enjoy my sweets somewhere much more exciting.

We took about two more steps before I pulled her hand, twirling her back around — piercing her hard nipples back into my chest.

I wanted Shay and I wanted her bad.

I placed my hands onto Shay's face and drew her lips back onto mine. I slid my tongue between her lips and kissed her passionately. As our tongues intertwined, I slowly unwrapped her satin robe and opened it, revealing her beautiful breasts in the midnight air.

Her nipples were hungry for my affection.

So, I leaned down and placed my lips onto her hard nipples, suckling on them as she moaned softly. I lifted my head and placed my lips back onto hers and massaged my palms onto her breasts, caressing them slowly. I guided my hands onto her shoulders and arms, and softly rubbed her goosebumps up and down. I slid my hands inside of her robe and relaxed them onto her hips.

Shay inhaled deeply.

When Shay exhaled, causing her body to relax, I traced my hands down to her waist, around her curves, and took two handfuls of her bouncy ass into my hands. I rubbed my hands in circular motions all over her ass, gripping and squeezing it at the cuffs.

Her skin was smooth like butter.

As I continued delivering passionate kisses on Shay's sexy lips and feeling on her booty, I turned her around and slowly walked her backwards toward the front of the car. When we reached the hood of my Camaro, I looked up and watched as the crescent moonlight shined down onto the hood of my car and lit up the water ripples in the horizon.

"Lick it Up Daddy"

Jameel Davis

With the moonlight shining onto the sparkling red paint like it was, I knew exactly where I wanted to bury my nose between her peanut butter chocolate thighs at— smelling her roses, as I French kissed her cocoa butter lips — sucking the slimy-vanilla-filling from deep inside of her.

I let go of Shay, removed my Puma hoodie, and spread it out on the hood of the car. Then, I kneeled down and wrapped my arms around Shay, placing my oven mitts on the back of her thighs. I stood up and lifted Shay up onto the hood of the car. Once I had her on the car, I laid her back on my hoodie with her thighs wide open, as if she was about to give birth.

"One second," I said. "I have to grab something out of the car."

"Ok," she replied.

I ran around to the driver side door, reached into my window, and retrieved the honey lemon-flavored Halls, and the sandwich bag that contained the cubes of ice. Some of the cubes had already melted, but I still had a few to work with.

"Lick it Up Daddy"

Jameel Davis

I unwrapped a Hall, popped it in my mouth, then opened the sandwich bag and popped a medium sized ice cube inside with it. I walked back to the front of the car and placed the sandwich bag on the hood of the car. I took control of Shay's buttery thighs, positioning her body so the crescent moonlight could shine bright onto her beautifully waxed and shiny vagina — while I ate it up.

Spotlight. Red Stage. Fifty Thousands Licks Twirling In A Maze...

I slowly inclined forward, bringing my thirsty mouth onto her thigh. I held the honey lemon-flavored HALL underneath my tongue and slowly kissed up and down her thighs.

Shay moaned quietly, anticipating my mouth to devour her cocoa butter lips.

I brought the ice to the opening of my lips and traced the cube in circular motions onto her inner thighs,getting it as close to her pussy as I could without touching her lips. Shay arched her back and drove her hips toward my face, searching for my cool lips and tongue. I held the melting ice between my tongue and lips, and gently twirled my lips and the ice up and down her thighs until the ice disappeared. The water raced down her thighs and onto her juicy chocolate lips. I placed my mouth onto her lips and slowly slurped the water up from them.

"Lick it Up Daddy"

Jameel Davis

Shay gasped loudly in pleasure, driving her pussy hard into my mouth.

I leaned back a bit and watched closely as Shay dug her fingertips into the hood of the car for support — grinding her hips, searching for my tongue to latch onto her clitoris once more.

When she couldn't fasten her throbbing clitoris onto my mouth, she relaxed her glazed milk chocolate buns back onto my hoodie.

As soon as her bottom touched the fabric, I quickly lifted my head to grab another cube of ice.

Before grabbing hold of the sandwich bag, I paused momentarily, taking in how pretty her pussy looked. Miss Pretty Pussy. Her pussy lips were glissing like my candy paint in the moonlight. It was one of the most exotic moments ever:

I had an elegant and sophisticated Black Woman; a Cinderella, dressed in a very sexy ivory robe, with buttery peanut butter and chocolate skin, who smelled so lovely lying on the hood of my brand new 2020 candy red Camaro — near the lake — with her legs open under the moonlight, — waiting for my lips to return to her freshly waxed, warm, and peachy pussy lips.

I had picked the perfect woman and the perfect place to satisfy my sweet tooth that night.

My dick is smiling right now thinking about it.

Shay's pussy was even more pulchritudinous in person. Not a mark, nor bump. Just pure, fresh, and smooth.

My wet mouth and the light from the moon had put an extra beam on her pussy, and it was time for me to make her pussy cream...

After placing another ice cube in my mouth, I watched Shay's clitoris throb rapidly for my cool mouth.

I retrieved the honey lemon-flavoredHalls from beneath my tongue and sucked on it with the ice as I lowered my head back down between her thighs, latching my soothing, cool, honey and lemon-flavored mouth right onto her warm and horny clitoris.

Shay quickly inhaled deeply and moaned loudly, exhaling her warm Spearmint breath into the midnight air. I twirled the ice and Halls on her clitoris with my mouth, then sucked on her clitoris, the ice and the Halls all-together sending a thrilling and soothing sensation deep into her drooling pussy.

"Lick it Up Daddy"

Jameel Davis

Shay quivered and let out a loud and sexy cry that echoed across the water.

"Oooshit."

"Ooo she missed you Daddy,: Shay moaned in a whisper after catching her breath.

I lifted my head from her clitoris, licked her juices off of my lips, and looked right into her eyes, "I Love You Too."

I bowed my head back inside of Shay's lap, held open her thighs with my oven mitts and got to licking and sucking away, melting the honey lemon-flavored Halls all over her melting lips and clitoris.
Shay moaned and moaned, squirming on the hood of the car, secreting a stream of clear gel onto the red paint.

My paint was extra wet. Shining like lipgloss.

I pulled the hood back off her clitoris and tasered it with my flickering tongue. Shay placed her hand softly on the back of my head and grinded her clitoris up against my lips. With each thrust, I French kissed her Puma, sucking away the slimy-cream-filling that was oozing from deep inside of her.

"Lick it Up Daddy"

Jameel Davis

My tastebuds were excited; they watered for more.

I lifted my mouth off of Shay's slimy pussy and licked up the sweet crystal like gel that was dangling from my bottom lip. I lifted my body up from the car and placed my hands on her hips, motioning for Shay to turn over to her stomach.

Shay turned over with her knees buried into my hoodie— Face Down, Ass Up, gripping the back end of the hood near the windshield.

I think Shay anticipated me climbing onto the hood of the car and digging my talented dick deep inside of her creamy-filled walls. But, that's not what I came to do. I wanted something sweet on my tongue to satisfy my midnight cravings and my treat was locked away deep inside of her.

The moonlight was now shining bright onto her glazed milk chocolate buns and all I needed was a glass of ice cold vanilla almond milk to pair with the creamy dessert I was getting ready to extract from inside her walls.

I placed another ice cube inside of my mouth and submerged my forehead and nose between her cheeks. I opened my mouth and slipped the ice cube inside of her hot pussy, and drove my tongue deep inside of her.

Shay took a deep breath, then hollered "Ooooshit," relaxing her torso onto the hood of the car.

Shay wagged her tail in excitement.

I alternated, stroking my tongue inside of her pussy, and suckling and licking on her delicious chocolate lips and hot pink clitoris.

Shay grinded her pussy harder and harder onto my lips, moaning and breathing heavily. Her breathing intensified as I licked her pussy and clitoris to the tune of Rock Me Baby, gradually increasing the speed and pressure of my tongue.

I felt Shay's body tense up and start to lose control. She was seconds away from showering my tastebuds with her deliciousness.

I sucked, nibbled, and licked — sucked, nibbled, and licked — faster and faster until she erupted her warm jelly-filled icing and the warm water from the ice cube she melted onto my warm, thirsty tongue.

Shay screamed once more into the calm night, this time much louder — releasing everything she had in her. Her moans wailed beautifully into the night sky.

I made love inside of her walls.

Shay was unable to move a muscle after climaxing inside of my mouth. She laid still with her face down, ass up taking in the moment of ecstasy. My tongue had paralized her whole body and my hoodie had fallen to the ground.

I gently kissed her sensitive lips and clitoris, and stood up from the car. Shay's pulchritudinous pussy was now glowing in the night and I watched as her juices dripped onto and flowed down the hood of my Camaro, like the waves in Lake Erie flowed to her shore. Shay smiled at me when she looked back at me. I wiped some of the vanilla frosting from her lips, sucked it off my fingers and smiled back.

So Delicious Girl.

Sex-Esteem
"Lick it Up Daddy"
Jameel Davis

Just Say You Want To *Fuck!*

You're grown, aren't you?

"Lick it Up Daddy"

Jameel Davis

I want to Fuck U...

How!? When? Where!?

Slowly and with passion tonight. My house...

I want to sit on your face, cum on your lips, and lick it all off. Then I want to stick my tongue in your mouth and let you suck the flavor off of my tongue. I want to hold you close to me as I grip my pussy lips and walls around your dick, squeezing you tighter and tighter with each slow thrust until my body contracts and quivers in ecstasy - making a delicious mess all over your dick. Cum with me and I promise to suck us all off of you.

"Lick it Up Daddy"

Jameel Davis

WAITING ON THE RAIN TO COME, SO I CAN WET YOUR SHEETS ONCE MORE.

"Lick it Up Daddy"

Jameel Davis

Sex-Esteem
Creme
whipping
"Whip it Up Daddy"
Jameel Davis

ACKNOWLEDGEMENTS

I would like to thank my fun, passionate and all-around family, friends and Street Team members for contributing their time, thoughts and ideas during the creation of this book and for helping me create buzz for Sex-Esteem. Some include; My mother Louise, Brandon, Kevin, Nee Nee, Jayson, Gerrell, Cierra, Latonya, Jayson, Alana, Amber, Tiffany, Octavia, Antonice, Whitney, Charkia, and a host of other relatives, friends, colleagues and supporters.

I would like to extend my gratitude to my Jamaican-Canadian literary friend and editor Stacey Robinson of Kya Publishing for delivering another phenomenal manuscript for my readers to enjoy. I would like to recognize my amazingly gifted illustrators and graphic designers, Michael Yeboah (West Africa, Ghana), Ashley Mae Pancho (Philippines) and Sana Liaqat for designing and curating the pages in this book with care, love, vibrant and beautiful erotica images for my readers to enjoy. A million thanks to my audience and supporters around the world for allowing me to light up their world with my knowledge, wisdom, professionalism, creativity, love and excitement. I wouldn't have made it to book number five without you all.

MORE BOOKS FROM CLEVELAND AUTHOR JAMEEL DAVIS

HOW SUCCESS BECAME MY FOCUS

CULTIVATING MINDS TO OWN THYSELF

IN BETWEEN THESE SHEETS

COMPLETELY NAKED

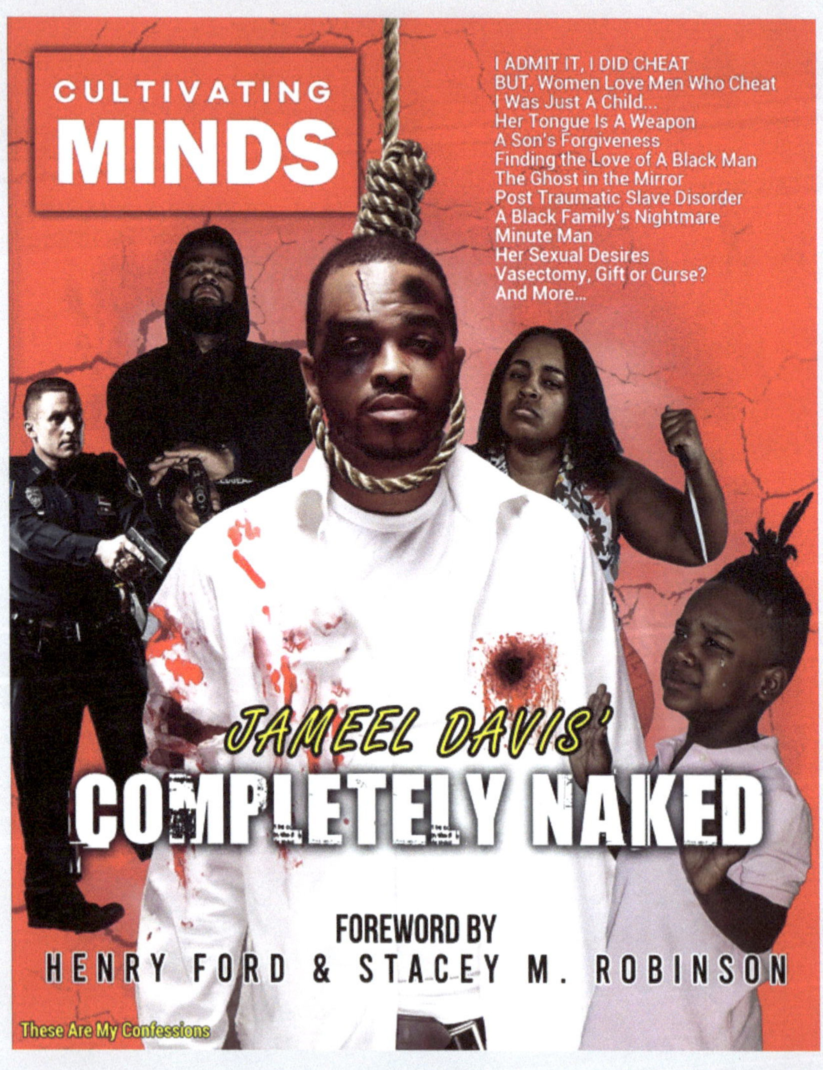

Coming Soon...

When I Grow Up I Wanna Be Just Like Me

Self-Awareness Is Uncomfortable But It's Sexy

TONIGHT I JUST WANNA GET DRUNK AND HAVE SOME WILD-CRAZY-SEX WITH BACK-TO-BACK ORGASMS.

Don't you?

DON'T SLEEP ON ME, SLEEP WITH ME!

#SEXESTEEM

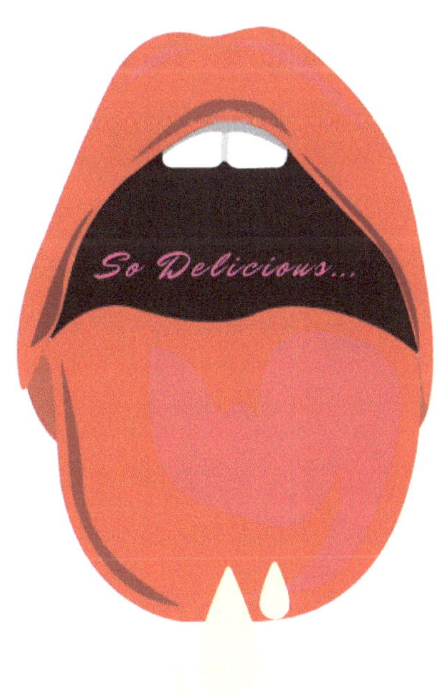

Jameel Davis